THE BAITED TRAP

by

Michael Limmer

'Hast thou found me, o mine enemy?'

1 Kings 21:20

This is a work of fiction, and accordingly parts of the city of Oxford and Oxfordshire countryside have been re-designed to fit the plot. All characters are drawn from the author's imagination and bear no relation to any persons living or dead.
It's fiction – enjoy it!

Mystery Thrillers from Michael Limmer

The Last Breath of Summer

Don't Start Now

A Heart to Betray

A Whisper in the Gloom

Past Deceiving

Marla

The Neal Gallian Trilogy

The Scars of Shame

The Relentless Shadow

The Baited Trap

All titles available in paperback and e-book via Amazon or from mike_limmer@yahoo.com

THE BAITED TRAP

PROLOGUE

Perhaps he was safe now…

These days, he felt safer than at that time before, but he was still continually looking over his shoulder, a latent fear his constant companion.

Although he was finished with Oxford, relieved that he had no reason to go back there. How he wished he'd never met Terry Arden, wished he hadn't allowed himself to be so easily influenced by him. It was a friendship which had ended disastrously for them both.

He felt that he'd drawn a line under it all, that he could start again. He was good at his job, found there were times when he could enjoy it, those times when he could store what had happened at the very back of his mind. It came down to a matter of continuing to go forward slowly, each day distancing him even further from those incidents in the past.

And yet, he couldn't help feeling that his troubles might not have ended with Arden's death. His first fear had been that Arden might have lived long enough to give away his name, his next that the police detective might have caught a glimpse of the fleeing car's numberplate on that fateful evening.

But no. Several months had passed since then, and there'd been no awkward questions. Every time he'd answered the telephone, he'd fought to keep his voice steady, feeling the cold wriggle of perspiration across his brow, quietly exhaling with relief when he'd recognized the voice as that of a customer or work colleague.

Each day he promised himself that he'd put it all behind him, get on with his life.

Because it might be, after all, that he was safe now.

Although he could never be entirely sure.

November 1964

1

Avril Walden, manageress of Paper, Pen & Ink in Oxford's High Street, waited as her colleague checked the nooks and crannies of the shop for stray customers. Once she'd given her the nod, Avril switched off the lights and the two women left the shop together, Avril locking the doors behind her. They exchanged goodnights and set off in opposite directions, Avril heading for Queen Street and a bus to take her home to Botley. It was a typically cold November evening, and she pulled up her coat collar as she walked and slipped on the gloves from her pocket. The streetlights threw back her reflection from the darkened shop windows, and Avril had to admit she didn't look bad for thirty-three, even after a busy day at work and even if she would look better for losing three or four pounds in weight.

Joining the queue, she huddled deeper into her coat to counter the biting wind but was warmed by thoughts of Bob. They'd never mentioned ages, but she knew he was a few years younger than her. And anyway, being with him helped her feel younger than her years. Avril felt a frisson of pleasure as she imagined Bob waiting at home for her, as opposed to Neville. It would make going home a delight rather than a chore. However, Bob was on the road with his job, and Avril wouldn't get to see him until the following week.

The bus was late, and the minutes dragged by. As she stood there, Avril started to feel uncomfortable, as if someone was watching her. But the two women behind were chatting away volubly, and on looking round Avril didn't think anyone was paying her undue attention.

Over to the right of the queue, several men were spread along the adjacent shop front, some squatting on the windowsill smoking or reading a newspaper. She caught the eye of one, a sly-looking little man in a rust-coloured suit and a stupid green hat with a feather. He gave back an oily smile and touched his hat in a mocking salute of acknowledgement. Avril hated being ogled and looked away with a shiver.

Finally, the bus pulled in, and Avril, aware of the man tagging on to the back of the queue, boarded it and quickly sat down next to an elderly woman. There were several double seats free, but she didn't want to run the risk of him plumping down next to her. Once he was on, he ambled past her down the aisle, and she lowered her gaze, her nostrils assaulted by the pungent smell of his cheap cologne. Without looking round, she sensed that he'd moved along towards the rear of the bus.

Traffic on the Botley Road was nose to tail, and the journey home took longer than usual. The bus made several stops to decant one or two passengers. To Avril's regret, the little man wasn't among them. She hoped he wasn't going to get off at her stop.

Arrived at Elms Parade, she was quickly out of her seat, one of the first to get off, and she hurried across the square and down the road which led to her estate. Realizing that the bus was yet to move off, she looked back and saw him framed in the doorway. He seemed to be staring after her. There was some distance between them, but even so Avril picked up her pace, heels clacking purposefully on the pavement.

A little way along, a narrow alley between two hedges offered a short cut through to her road. She seldom took it, particularly after dark, but now she plunged down it and, reaching the end, paused and looked back again. She gasped as she saw his squat figure in the opening, sinisterly silhouetted beneath a streetlamp's feeble glow.

Avril's heart pounded as she hurried on. *Who was he? What did he want with her?* She couldn't bear to contemplate an answer to those questions. It was definitely her he was following, her and nobody else. She shook her head disbelievingly. *No – surely, surely this couldn't be happening...*

At last, she found herself in her road. Peering desperately down it, she saw a light shining dimly behind the living room curtains. It meant that Neville was there, and she felt a little less afraid. Neville – her saviour! She could scarcely believe it but was willing to settle for it in her present predicament.

Avril scuttled down the road, through her gate and on to the garden path before taking another look back. She saw no sign of her pursuer and sighed with relief. Had her anxiety, fear, been unreasonable? Perhaps he hadn't been following her after all? Maybe he was just one of those perverted men who got his kicks from making women feel uncomfortable, that he didn't mean any real harm?

Approaching the front door, Avril fumbled the key from her handbag, almost dropping it as she inserted it into the lock. It was sticking a bit as it turned, and she pushed against the door, a chill racing through her being as she heard footsteps on the pavement, light with menace. Her fears rushed in upon her, for he must have been right behind her after all, and with a stifled gasp she pushed against the door with all her strength, tripping over the step and just managing to save herself from falling headlong into the hallway.

She swung round to find that he wasn't there and, crazy with relief, slammed the door shut, reassured by the snap of the Yale lock as it closed. She stood for a few moments, leaning against the hallstand for support, her racing heartbeat slowly returning to normal.

In the new silence, Avril heard the familiar rustle of a newspaper from the living room, followed by Neville's voice. "That you, Av?"

Who else did he think it was? Neville was always capable of changing her mood for the worse, but at least his presence offered a temporary respite from her recent fear.

"Yes, it's me," she replied wearily, as she peeled off her coat and hung it on the hallstand.

Following the creak of a spring, Neville's large, tousled head appeared round the living room door. "Expected you home before now," he grumbled.

She recited the usual litany of excuses. "I had to lock up the shop, the bus was late, and we were queued from before we got to the station." *And there was a man following me, as if you'd care,* she thought about adding.

As usual, there was no sympathy to be had from Neville. "Well, I need to be off to work soon. Could do with some tea."

Avril bit back a sharp retort. "I'll get on with it right away," she conceded grudgingly.

Satisfied, Neville's head withdrew, the armchair's spring twanged, and the newspaper rustled again.

Back to drudgery. Work could be a bind at times, particularly with the occasional awkward customer, but Avril would take it every time over *this*. Kicking off her heels, she wriggled her feet into slippers, tied on her apron and was about to re-acquaint herself with her eternal kitchen, when a folded sheet of paper slid through the letterbox and plopped onto the mat. She snatched it up quickly and stuffed it into her apron pocket, as Neville's chair gave another creak and the newspaper was slapped down onto the arm, heralding the reappearance of his head round the door.

"What you hanging about for, then?"

"For goodness' sake, Neville. I've just this minute got in."

"Well, time's getting on. I'll soon have to be -."

"Yes, I know. I'll sort it out now."

With a theatrical sigh, Avril disappeared into the kitchen and busied herself preparing a fry-up, always his favourite, although the washing-up would carve a swathe out of her evening. Still, feed him and get him gone, clear it all away and she'd have some time to herself.

He came slouching in after her second call, *Oxford Mail* in one hand and dragging out one of the kitchen chairs with the other, the back legs digging into the lino. He sank down on to it with a graceless thump and muttered "Ta" as she set a loaded plate before him. He slathered ketchup over it and propped the paper up against the bottle, effectively creating a screen between them and killing conversation.

As she sat opposite, picking at her food, listening to him chomping away and slurping his tea, Avril wondered what she'd ever seen in him. They'd been married for nine years. There were no kids. She'd have liked them, but he'd been adamant from early on that he didn't want any, and once he'd given up playing rugby he'd started to put on weight. He never helped with household chores – *"What d'you think I've got a wife for?"* – and only showed an interest in her when he rolled back from the pub on a Saturday night. There was no romance in their marriage. Perhaps, Avril thought soberly, it had only ever existed in her mind.

With a final, echoing belch, Neville shoved back his chair and stood up. "Thanks, Av. Needed that." He snatched up the paper and planted a greasy kiss on her cheek. "Better get changed and shoot off."

She smiled wanly, finished her meal and had started on the washing-up by the time he came thundering down the stairs. He leaned through into the kitchen, head and shoulders this time, not just the head. Something important, then.

"Av, this bloke might phone about a car I'm doing up for him. Take his number and say I'll get back to him at the weekend, right? See you in the morning."

When he'd come whistling into the bedroom – her alarm clock – and demand a mug of tea and toast before she could get herself ready and leave for work. *Ships that pass in the night, or early morning.* Not much of a marriage, but Avril was beginning to prefer it the way it was.

She'd reckoned he might have had enough of cars, what with his night shift at the factory. Still, while he was working away in his garage or round at his mate Stan's and then down at the pub, it meant that she didn't see a lot of him.

Once he'd left, and Avril had washed and dried up and was sitting in the living room with a reviving mug of tea, she suddenly remembered the note, still nestling in her apron pocket. She took it out, unfolded and read it.

And her eyes widened in horror at the words and what they meant for her.

2

If ever there was a picture of utter misery, it was the sight of Detective Chief Inspector Don Pilling which greeted his colleagues Sergeant Tom Wrightson and Detective Sergeant Neal Gallian, as they were shown into his living room. The shirt-sleeved Pilling was leaning back resignedly in his armchair with one heavily bandaged foot resting on a pouffe and a walking-stick abandoned resentfully on the floor beside him.

Sheila, the DCI's long-suffering wife, showed the visitors to seats. "Make yourselves comfortable, gentlemen," she invited them, "and I'll put the kettle on."

Pilling turned his head as the sound of voices penetrated his gloomy thoughts. "Ah!" he exclaimed. "Sanity at last, and a double dose of it."

Neal could tell their boss was glad to see them, even though it didn't register on his face. But happiness seldom did. A wiry, experienced detective in his late forties, Don Pilling was a hard taskmaster, and for his part Neal wouldn't have had it any other way. As a constable, he'd been wounded in a shooting in which his best friend Clyde Holt had been killed. Once he'd recovered, he'd quit the force but, having been caught up in a case involving several murders in the late summer of the previous year, he'd run across the DCI and had been persuaded to return. Pilling had wanted him in CID, and he'd started as a detective constable, but within a few months Pilling's long-term sidekick, DS Thackray, had suffered a serious illness. Neal had been promoted to Acting DS and, now that Thackray had taken early retirement and moved to the south coast for the sake of his health, had passed the relevant exams to become a full detective sergeant. He had a lot to thank Don Pilling for and resolved to show his gratitude by doing the job well.

He placed a few back copies of *Rugby World* on the coffee table next to the DCI's chair. "Jill's uncle thought you might appreciate these, Guv. He doesn't need them back."

Pilling responded with a nod. "Thank him for me, will you, Neal? It'll be good to have something decent to read. The papers are full of doom and gloom – all about another vote of no confidence in the government. And as for television – pah!"

This was only Neal's second visit to the Pillings' neat semi in Headley Way, simply because he never usually saw his boss anywhere other than at the station. Pilling had been cleaning the bedroom windows the previous weekend, when he'd slipped off the ladder and suffered a badly sprained ankle, keeping him off work and under doctor's orders, neither of which suited him.

Sheila bustled in with the tray, arranged cups and plates on the coffee table, passed round chocolate digestives and poured tea. She was a short, energetic woman of infinite patience and irrepressible cheerfulness.

"It's so thoughtful of you both to drop in," she declared. "Donald's been sitting there, practically tearing his hair out. The doctor's calling again in the middle of next week, and we hope it'll be good news for both our sakes. To think I criticized Donald for spending so little time at home! Didn't know when I was well off, did I? This last week has felt like a year."

Pilling rolled his eyes, gritting his teeth to contain his exasperation. "For crying out loud, Sheila! You know darned well I'd rather not be sitting around here twiddling my thumbs."

"Temper, temper, Donald." With a prim smile, Sheila calmly handed round the biscuits again. "Well, now," she resumed. "I dare say you men will want to talk shop, so I'll make myself scarce. Call me if you need anything else."

Pilling waited, unnecessarily in Neal's opinion, until the door had closed. At a nod from Tom, he pitched in.

"We assumed you'd want an update, Guv, although there's not a lot to report. It's been mainly routine stuff, although you'll be pleased to know the burglaries in Wolvercote aren't a problem any longer. Last night, a resident heard a noise from the house next door and, knowing full well that his neighbours were away on holiday, he called us. Hodgson and Palgrave went round and collared Barry Dillon in the act of lifting a sack load of expensive jewellery."

If it had been his habit, Pilling might have smiled. "That's a good result, lads. It'll be good to have Dillon out of our hair for a while."

"And that's not all, Guv," Neal went on. "You know Dillon. If he's going down, he'll always make sure someone goes with him. He only handed us Solly Bremmer – on a plate."

Pilling arched his capacious eyebrows. "Well, well," he purred. "All good things come to those who wait. Solly's been fencing stolen goods for years and always managed to slither out of our clutches. This is getting better and better. What's next?"

"Just me putting the dampers on it, Don," Tom Wrightson put in with a grin. Neal had hardly ever seen the bluff, balding Yorkshireman out of uniform, but tonight he was smartly turned out in blazer, crisp white shirt and flannels for this not-quite-social call. He and the DCI had been colleagues and friends for years, but Tom, a stickler for protocol, would only ever address Pilling as 'sir' when on duty. "Your friend Larry Rackham's been sniffing around. Ingratiating himself with one or two of our junior colleagues to see what he can get out of them. Everyone's been told not to give him the time of day. Whenever he shows up, he's to speak to me and no-one else. And if I find anyone's been talking out of turn, he or she'll be in trouble."

"That's the way, Tom," the DCI concurred. "Rackham's a pain in the nether regions and needs to be kept in his place, like every blasted journalist. How's young Palgrave shaping up, by the way? To my mind, he seems to be the best of the new intake."

"Coming along okay. I've put him on the cars with Hodgson this week, and WPC Begley will walk him through his beat next week. The gap left by Thomas is going to be a big one to fill, but Dakers and the WPC contingent are more than pulling their weight, as you'd expect. As Neal said, there's not a lot going on at present, and we should be thankful for small mercies."

"You're coping, then?"

"Pretty much, I'd say."

"I knew you would. If the time came when I couldn't rely on you two, we might as well shut up shop and go home."

"You are home, Don," Wrightson grinned.

Pilling grimaced, casting a quick glance towards the door. "Yes, and don't I ruddy know it." He looked from one to the other as they sat drinking their tea. "Well, lads, I'm grateful for the update. But that's not the main reason I'm glad you dropped by." His face suddenly darkened, as if he was fighting to control an outburst.

"I had the ACC on the blower this morning." Pilling strove to keep his voice level. Assistant Chief Constable Clive Streatley had always been capable of riling him, often merely by existing. "A ruddy stuffed shirt if ever there was one. He's not pleased with me for making my views known, and I'm blowed if I'm pleased with him. You'll be aware that I don't intend staying off work longer than I can help. It was my intention that you two would run the show in my absence – heaven knows you're capable enough. Don't get me wrong, Neal. The ACC's impressed with your contribution, but in his wisdom, he reckons it's too soon for you to have a spell as Acting Detective Inspector, however brief. So, he's arranged for a DI to be drafted in to oversee the station."

Tom Wrightson, looking affronted, shifted in his seat.

"Oh, it gets worse, Tom. It's Winter, and he's starting on Monday."

Tom groaned. "My feelings exactly," Pilling added.

"I take it that's Phil Winter, Guv?" Neal inquired.

"Of course, you wouldn't have known him." Winter had spent eighteen months at Oxford during the period Neal had been out of action. "He was keen, and I couldn't fault his work rate, but too quick to take whatever credit might be going. While he was with us, he got made up to DI and leapt at the chance when a secondment to the Met came up. To tell the truth, I was glad to get shot of him. The ACC, as you'd guess, liked him – university education and all that – and he's solely responsible for bringing him back. Reckons it'll be good experience. *'Just the sort of solid chap to run the show, Pilling, what?'*" Both his colleagues grinned at the DCI's take-off of his superior's plummy voice. "But at least he's agreed that the minute I can put weight on this confounded ankle, I'll be back."

Neal wondered if the ACC had bowed to that simply to allow himself to get off the phone. The prospect of Don Pilling in full rant wasn't an attractive one if you happened to be on the receiving end.

"You'll be wanting us to keep you in the picture till then, Don," Tom said, already sure of the answer.

"Yes, please, Tom. I'll be insisting on daily reports from Winter too, although he'll only tell me the bits he wants me to hear."

Neal found himself nodding in agreement. He wasn't altogether comfortable about going behind Phil Winter's back, because Winter would be his superior, and it would be down to him to report back to the DCI. On the other hand, Pilling was relying on him and Tom, and Neal owed the resurrection of his career to Pilling. "You can count on us, Guv," he heard himself saying.

Unseen by Pilling, a young tabby cat had sidled into the room, as the door hadn't been completely fastened. It made a beeline for him, and in one graceful movement had leapt up and made itself comfortable on his lap.

"Sheila!" Pilling exploded, snatching up the animal and dumping it unceremoniously on the floor. "Will you get this perishing thing away from me and sling it back outside where it belongs!"

Sheila Pilling hurried in, tut-tutting and shaking her head. "Honestly, the man has no patience at all. Beats me how you two manage to put up with him."

Neal, grinning, wondered how Sheila did, too. He also wondered if she might just have forgotten to properly close the living room door, allowing the cat to wander in…

Once his wife and pet had left the room, Pilling promised his colleagues that he'd continue to give the ACC earache over the matter, about which, as they'd gathered, he was far from pleased. "I shall certainly be redoubling my efforts to get mobile and back to work." It surprised Neal that ACC Streatley, a comfortable man steeped in formal dinners and rounds of golf, had gone against the DCI's wishes regarding the installation of Phil Winter, but he supposed that with Pilling a prisoner in his own home, he temporarily enjoyed the upper hand.

Neal and Tom wished their Guv'nor a speedy recovery, shook his hand and went out into the hallway where Sheila intercepted them. She thanked them for coming and told them they could pop round at any time.

"You may not believe it, but this evening's been a tonic for him. Oh, and Neal, do give Jill my love. I take it you're both settling down to married life? I thought your little flat looked lovely – your wife's such a talented girl." Thoughtful as ever, Jill had invited Sheila and Doreen Wrightson to tea a couple of weeks previously.

Once they were outside, Tom, realizing Neal was on foot, offered him a lift home.

"Thanks, Tom. But I'm just popping round to St Oswald's to meet Jill from choir practice. She's parked the car there."

"All going along okay, then?"

"Couldn't be better. Good to come home to a decent meal at night. I realize I spent too long eating out of tins."

Tom chuckled. "Aye, it's the way to a man's heart, make no mistake. Part of the reason I've been happily wed these twenty-odd years." Then his expression grew serious, and he drew Neal to one side.

"Listen, lad, keep a weather eye on Phil Winter. He's a decent enough boy but can be a bit gung-ho, which is what got the DCI's goat in the first place. And he's a mite too quick to take the glory. Now he's up to DI, I'd be worried the elevated rank might go to his head." He sighed. "The minute the DCI's back in harness, the better it'll be for the lot of us."

3

It was a twenty-minute walk into Headington, and Neal was glad to get into the relative warmth of the church, to be greeted by the unmistakable strains of the Hallelujah Chorus. He sat down in one of the middle pews, the first time he'd relaxed that day. Jill stood in the choir's front row. She'd always had a love of singing, and the choirmaster had been enthusiastic about the addition of another soprano to their ranks. Neal watched her dreamily.

He recalled their wedding two months previously, becoming immune, as the date approached, to wisecracks from people like his colleague DC Mal Brady. *"You're about to lose your freedom, Gally. Got that look about you like a man on his way to the scaffold."* Even the DCI had got in on the act with a lugubrious *"There'll be no going back, you know. Look what it's done to me."* Yes, that had been a sobering thought.

Although Neal had never seen it that way. He and Jill, at the time of their wedding, had known each other for little more than a year. They'd been attracted to one another from their first meeting: two shy, lonely people grateful for each other's understanding and company. There was a bit of an age gap: she was twenty-three and he thirty-four. But that didn't bother Neal, for Jill had an old head on young shoulders.

Taff Thomas was his best man, and they'd both been on edge as they'd stood waiting at the altar. *"You did remember to bring the ring, didn't you, Taff?" "That's the fifth time you've asked me in the last half-hour, boyo. Bit nervous, are you?" "Just a bit." "Makes two of us, then. And, yes, I've got the ring – I think."*

Neal had known Taff a while. They'd both transferred to Oxford when they'd been young constables six or seven years previously and had got on well from the outset. The genial Welshman had always been a bit of a lad, but he was a staunch friend and good policeman who'd not at all resented Neal's return to the force and rapid promotion to Detective Sergeant. Indeed, he'd passed his own sergeants' exam earlier in the year and was currently working as station sergeant in nearby Abingdon.

Neal was glad of Taff's support and friendship over the wedding, as he had no family at all. His brother had died in the war, and his parents had passed on in recent years. Taff had, according to tradition, arranged Neal's stag night for the eve of the wedding. Knowing that Neal enjoyed a drink, although never to excess, Taff had thoughtfully made the occasion an 'open house', when all their colleagues and friends had been invited to drop into a nearby pub after work to wish the prospective groom health and happiness. Everyone, even Mal Brady, behaved impeccably, particularly when the DCI was present, and only Neal and Taff were left at the end, with the latter the only casualty of the evening, drinking steadily, bemoaning the current lack of a girlfriend and altogether becoming quite maudlin.

But he was at Neal's door in good time the next morning to drive him to Braxbury church. It seemed they'd been waiting for hours, conscious of the pews filling up behind them, when the organ had suddenly shrilled into the Wedding March, and he turned to see a radiant Jill walking up the aisle on her father's arm. They made their vows to one another, words spoken solemnly, gazes locked together and eyes full of meaning, and he felt the love shone from hers even more brightly than when she'd sat beside his hospital bed and kept her long, faithful vigil the year before.

At the wedding breakfast in Braxbury village hall, both Jill's dad and Taff made mercifully brief and generous speeches in the couple's honour. Neal had wondered what Taff might have come up with from the past, but it was nothing more embarrassing than an incident from early in Neal's career when he'd attended to an elderly lady who'd fallen in Oxford's Cornmarket Street. He'd dusted her down and driven her home, only to discover days later that she was one of the city centre's most notorious shoplifters, and that the basket Neal had kindly carried to her door was full of that day's haul from the Oxford shops. There'd been worse embarrassments, but Taff had tastefully left them out in deference to the memory of Clyde Holt, Neal's best friend and colleague. Clyde would likely have been on patrol with Neal at those times, and he was to die later in the shooting which had seen Neal badly wounded.

His own blundering testimony didn't stand comparison with those which had gone before, and his account of how meeting Jill had changed his life for the better held all the appeal of one of his reports to the DCI, but the applause he received from the gathering truly astounded him. He thought perhaps people were just glad that the speeches were over. The dancing which followed was a source of great amusement, not least the sight of Neal's slightly tipsy colleagues, WPCs Yvonne and Pam, dragging Jill's correct, ex-military uncle, Lambert Wilkie, on to the dance floor in a loose rendition of the Twist and Bossa Nova.

Neal spent some time with Flo and Ron Ormsby, the couple with whom he'd lodged when he'd been stationed at Cirencester. Ron, looking spiv-like and undernourished in his ill-fitting suit, had only come for the beer, but Flo had been transported by the occasion. "Oh, Neal my duck, Jill looks *so* lovely. Please, please don't forget to come down and see us." Neal promised faithfully that they wouldn't, for Jill had been virtually adopted by the childless Flo. "Such a *dear* girl. I took to her the minute I set eyes on her." Ron, being Ron, was more of an acquired taste, nodding away as if in full agreement between slurps of brown ale.

Jill's parents, Ben and Janet Westmacott, bronzed from their years spent beneath the African sun, cheerfully did the rounds alongside the bride and groom, while the merriment continued in full swing. Sheila Pilling and Doreen Wrightson jived away together, having given up on their impervious husbands. The DCI had snorted derisively and taken refuge in his pipe, while Tom had sent Doreen on her way with a dismissive "If you're determined to make a fool of yourself, lass, go right ahead. But count me out." Even the prowling Yvonne and Pam didn't have the temerity to try to get their superiors on their feet.

Taff, meanwhile, had been catapulted out of any gloom lingering from the previous evening by his first sight of Jill's young bridesmaid, her cousin Ella, with blonde tresses halfway down her back and a sylph-like frame. "Looks like she just walked out of a ruddy dream, boyo," he confided in an aside to Neal. "I'd better hold off on the juice in case she might appreciate a lift home later."

Neal and Jill were glad to see that his colleague and her friend WDC Sally Dakers had paired up with PC Paul Hodgson, and they seemed to be having a good time in each other's company. Sally had let down her red hair and looked quite striking.

Old boots and horseshoes had been tied to the back bumper of Neal's car, as everyone gathered to cheer them off on a week's honeymoon in Devon. Jill pitched her bouquet into Sally's arms, tradition indicating that she'd be next to wed. The return to their flat the following Saturday saw

Neal carry his bride over two thresholds to the delight and applause of their elderly downstairs neighbours, Mr and Mrs Stone.

Lost in this reverie, Neal had been alerted by the nearby buzz of voices that choir practice was over. He looked up to find Jill advancing towards him, bright, cheerful and welcoming, and he rose to greet her with a kiss and help her into her coat. He noticed one or two older choir members watching them indulgently. *"You can tell they're not long married. He's even come to meet her."*

As they walked out to where she'd left the car, Jill asked how DCI Pilling was faring?

"Just as I'd expected," he replied. He's bored out of his skull and bad-tempered with it. Sheila should be recommended for sainthood."

Jill squeezed his hand and looked up at him adoringly. "I'm sure you'll never be like that."

He chuckled. "And I'm sure you'd let me know if I was."

Jill had worked hard on transforming their very ordinary little flat. She'd made and fitted patterned curtains and repainted the walls in various pastel colours. The doors and window frames gleamed with white gloss. She and Neal had received much-needed furniture as wedding gifts: a pair of armchairs to complement the sofa Neal had provided, as well as a living room carpet and new cooker. Fittingly, Colonel Wilkie had bought them the cooker, a nod to Jill's culinary skills, for she'd lived with and looked after him for several years, while her parents, both teachers, were out in Kenya.

The Westmacotts and Wilkie professed themselves delighted with the flat, and Jill, ever mindful of her uncle's generosity – he'd always treated her like the daughter he and his late wife had never had – had agreed with Neal that she'd call in on him a couple of times each week to cook, clean and generally keep his house in order. She and Neal would also go out one Sunday each month to share a Sunday roast with him. Wilkie would certainly miss his niece, but he had local friends who were ex-servicemen and would often be away for a couple of days at a time at what he and his cronies termed 'reunion' dinners.

Ben and Janet had stayed with him for a couple of weeks after the wedding before going back to Kenya, and they'd decided to return to

England the following year and settle somewhere in the Oxfordshire countryside.

"Surely Mr Pilling's going to be out of action for a while?" Jill remarked, as they settled down that evening to cocoa and a light supper.

"It's partly why we were summoned there this evening," Neal replied. "And partly why he's in such a thundering bad mood. The ACC has insisted on bringing in a Detective Inspector to oversee the station in his absence, and the Guv'nor's not impressed with his choice. It's a chap named Phil Winter, who was there for over a year while I was absent. He's on a secondment to the Met, and I gather he's very ambitious. Tom wasn't over the moon about it either. I've never met DI Winter, so don't know what to expect, except that he's bound to have a different approach from what we're used to. Still, I don't think anything's likely to keep the DCI away for long. In fact, he's probably determined to return sooner than we might have expected. Anything to spite the ACC."

4

Bob Sanderson was in a good mood. But then, he always was these days. He was a company representative, working for the Cheltenham-based firm, X-Pressive Stationery Supplies, and the good mood had kicked in that day back in early May when his sales manager, Mike Braddon, had called him into his office.

Bob was the youngest and most junior member of the sales team. He'd been with X-Pressive, or X-P as it was popularly known, for less than two years. He got on well with Braddon, who was something of a father figure to his 'boys', and with all the other reps, except one.

It had been back in May, six months previously, when Braddon had reallocated the sales areas. The most senior rep had recently retired, and it made sense that Jack Lumsden, who was next in line, should take over London and the South-East, by far the most important sales patch.

This left the second most lucrative area, the South Midlands, free, and Braddon had first offered it to Gordon Childers, who'd supervised Bob Sanderson's training. Childers, however, had turned it down, opting to stay with Wales and the North-West, a bigger patch which involved a lot of travelling.

Gordon had recommended Bob. He realized Bob was the least experienced member of the team but, having overseen his training, he was sure his young colleague would make a success of it.

Braddon had trusted Gordon's judgement and made Bob the offer, which had been accepted with alacrity and a measure of disbelief. The other reps, including Jack Lumsden, who'd been around a while, endorsed the appointment, acknowledging that Bob had what it took to become a good rep. But it had never gone down well with Tony Swires.

Discussing the matter privately with Bob, because the two men had become good friends, Gordon Childers wondered if Swires had expected to be offered the South Midlands area. It had been his patch a couple of years or more previously, and he'd been pulled out of it abruptly, for reasons which only he and Braddon knew, and had transferred to the South-West, swapping areas with Lumsden.

Not that Tony Swires was likely to confide in anyone. A beanpole of a man in his early thirties, he went around with a permanent chip on his shoulder, considering himself a better salesman than anyone else in the team. He hadn't taken Braddon's decision kindly and was often little short of rude to Bob and the mild-mannered Gordon Childers.

Their response was to keep out of his way as much as possible, which was difficult on those occasions when Braddon called the reps in for a sales meeting, or if they happened to be in the office on the same day as Swires.

Where possible, they'd give their prickly colleague a wide berth, sometimes meeting up for a quiet drink or dinner before heading home. On the last such occasion in early November, Gordon had confided that he'd recently purchased a small cottage in the Welsh Marches, partly why he'd turned down Mike Braddon's offer of the South Midlands. He was a keen hiker in his spare time, and the area offered him a lot of scope.

"Can't help thinking there might be a lady friend in the equation," Bob replied with a smile. "You'd have made a great success of the South Midlands."

"I prefer it where I am, Bob," Gordon said equably. "Lady friend or no lady friend, I'm drawn to the area where I live, and I enjoy visiting our accounts in the Welsh towns and cities. Perhaps I should have been born Welsh. And talking of lady friends, one or two colleagues have remarked that there seems to be a spring in *your* step these days. I know the job's going well – Mike seemed mightily impressed with your latest figures – but we suspect that's not the only reason."

Bob was unable to contain his happiness. "Well, I -er, met this lady, you see, Gordon. She manages the Paper, Pen & Ink shop in Oxford. She's really lovely – a Doris Day lookalike. She's a few years older than me, but I don't care about that."

Gordon sat stroking his beard, smiling indulgently at his friend's enthusiasm. "Sounds as though we might be hearing the sound of wedding bells before long, Bob?"

Bob hesitated, his expression clouding. "Er, well, Gordon, that's the difficulty. She's -er, married, you see. But far from happy. I think that at some stage – well, I hope she may be free."

Gordon was trying to look encouraging, but he'd always been a bit prudish, and Bob could tell he didn't really approve. "I'm sure you know what you're doing, Bob," he said. "But all I'd say is, tread carefully."

"I will. I mean, I'm not exactly shouting it around. You're the only person I've told."

"Then I'd advise you to leave it there, my friend. You know how word has a habit of spreading."

"I'll do that, Gordon. And thanks for the advice. I appreciate it."

The subject was changed, Gordon moving on to talk about his recent hike along a section of the Offa's Dyke Path. As he droned on, Bob's mind was on another matter, and he hoped his expression wasn't giving him away. There'd been some letters from Avril, and he'd been reading the latest one when Mike Braddon had happened along. He'd hastily stuffed it into his desk drawer.

He realized with horror that it was probably still there, and he'd need to retrieve it as soon as possible. There'd been a rumour going round about the time of his appointment to the South Midlands area, that Tony Swires wasn't above riffling through the other reps' desk drawers if he happened to be alone in the office, always with the ready excuse that he'd been looking for a pencil sharpener or an eraser. He wouldn't want Swires getting to know about him and Avril.

Although having mentioned her, as Gordon rambled comfortably on, he couldn't get the thought of her out of his head. He spent the rest of the evening in a dream, bolstered by the knowledge that he'd be seeing her again in a couple of days' time.

They met in Oxford University Parks. It was her day off, and he'd phoned her at the shop earlier in the week to say he'd be passing through on his way to an appointment in Banbury. Her voice had seemed strained and distant, but he'd put that down to her having a shop full of customers and unable to stay on the phone for long. He knew, too, that she'd not let any of her colleagues in on the news of their friendship.

He found her sitting primly on a park bench in fur coat, hat and boots, huddled against the cold weather. "Avril!" He strode towards her with arms outstretched, and she rose and turned towards him, almost collapsing into his embrace. He knew immediately that something was wrong, and alarm bells began to ring. On every previous occasion she'd been so pleased to see him, her face radiant with welcome. Might it possibly be that she'd tired of him? Might her husband have found out about them?

"Avril, darling – whatever's the matter?"

She looked up at him pitifully. So tall and handsome with his wavy blond hair, like some hero out of one of her Mills & Boon romances – and yet really so young and vulnerable. So gentle when he held her in his arms, as if he was afraid she might break... Avril's heart went out to him.

"Oh, Bob, I-I'm so sorry." She couldn't hold back her tears, and Bob, his face ashen, eyes wild with concern, steered her back to the bench and sat beside her, held her closely as she cried out her hurt. People walking by stared at them curiously, but he paid them no heed. Avril held all his attention and concern.

She'd reached into her handbag and taken something out, and now he prised it from between her fingers. He unfolded it and glanced over the words, his eyes widening in shock and disgust as he read them.

"But who – who sent this?" he stammered.

Avril took a small cotton handkerchief from her sleeve and dabbed at her tears. She sat for a few moments, still with his arms encircling her, aware of his anxious eyes as she tried to collect herself.

"I don't know his name."

Haltingly, Avril went on to recall that night over a week ago, when she'd been queueing for a bus in Queen Street and had noticed the odious little man watching her. She told Bob how he'd followed her off the bus, how she'd hurried home, quickening her pace for fear that he might be planning to attack her – how things might have been better if that had been all he'd had in mind. She told him how she'd got indoors only for that hateful note to drop onto the mat, of her anguish as she'd read it, the bottom threatening to fall out of her world.

"Then you've – paid him?" Bob asked, once she'd finished.

Avril nodded, yes.

She recalled her trepidation two long nights later. Neville, thankfully, had been at work. Avril had caught a bus along Botley Road, and she recounted stumbling into the Osney churchyard, its dim lighting, the night full of shadows. *"Third row of gravestones. Leave it in a carrier bag third row along,"* the note had instructed her, and she squelched across the grass, the gravestones like rows of mis-shapen, blackened teeth, fear wriggling through her whole being, chilling her almost into paralysis.

There'd been a rustling in the bushes just beyond her. She gasped. Was he there? A screech as a cat dashed out, chased by another. No, not there, but she knew he couldn't be far away. He'd told her the time to make the drop, and she'd arrived at the time he'd said, so he'd be watching, he'd have arrived early and would be well hidden.

She shivered uncontrollably, but not through the cold of the evening. For the idea had come upon her that this might be his time, the place and opportunity to assault her. To strangle her? Rigid with fear, helpless and alone, Avril let fall the carrier bag from her grasp at the spot he'd indicated and hurried away, not daring to look back as she lurched out of the churchyard and onto the street, out at last into the lights of the Botley Road. She got on the first bus which happened along, sank down onto a seat and longed for home, even for Neville to be there waiting, although she knew he wouldn't be.

"But Avril, why haven't you told the police?"

She smiled up at Bob wanly, reassured by his concern, pitying him for his innocence.

"Because he knows about us, my darling, and he's unscrupulous enough to let Neville know. And if Neville ever finds out, he'll beat me black and blue, particularly when he comes home rolling drunk on a Saturday night. Oh, Bob, I can't bear the thought of not being able to see you. You've changed my life – you mean so much to me."

Her tears fell again, and he held her closer still, stemming them now with his own handkerchief.

"And you've changed mine, Avril." He spoke boldly, with all the experience of his twenty-six years. "I love you. D'you hear me? I *love* you, and I – I - well, I'd *kill* myself if I thought I'd never see you again. But this man, he – he's a blackmailer. He'll -?"

"Yes." Her voice was steadier now. Bob would stand by her, she was sure of that. And she felt stronger for it, even though her fear, her foreboding, wouldn't go away. "Yes, he'll be in touch again. That one payment – it won't be the end of it."

"No, of course it won't. But next time I'll come with you." She started to protest, but as she looked up, she could see that she wouldn't dissuade him. Determination was set in every line of his face, and he spoke fiercely, her saviour and protector.

"Yes, Avril. I'll come with you. As soon as he makes contact, you must telephone me. You're more important to me than anything or anyone else, and no-one's going to stop me from seeing you. I'll come with you and sort him out, I promise you. Sort him out once and for all."

5

Jerry Rudd might not have been a murderer, but he was practically everything else. All his life he'd studiously avoided work, because crime came so naturally to him. He was a cheat, thief, conman, blackmailer, an opportunist always with an eye to the main chance and without a care for anyone who might get hurt, financially or otherwise along the way, as long as he remained in the clear.

He inhabited a room in a shabby, three-storey Victorian terraced house behind the railway station, a room replete with all sorts of items he'd stolen or conned from people. His philosophy was that these items now belonged to him, possession being nine-tenths of the law, and he'd only sell them if times got hard: the silver carriage clock on the mantelpiece, the diamond necklace stowed away at the back of his bedside drawer, the tall vase over in the corner – the old darling for whom he'd promised to get it valued had been sure it was Ming dynasty. It was a shame he kept forgetting to take it back to her, although she'd been on her last legs then and had probably kicked the bucket by now, so he'd sort of inherited it.

His landlady, Mrs Lynch, was the permanent soft touch, a decent old bird who'd taken in lodgers to help pay the way after her husband had died. She was as blind as a bat into the bargain, and Jerry took full advantage of that.

"Oh, Mr Rudd, have you seen that nice carving set of mine? I can't find it anywhere, and it was a wedding present from my uncle." So – it *was* an antique.

"Sorry, Mrs L. But remember you had that old gipsy bloke in sharpening knives the other week. He seemed a bit of a shifty one to me."

"Oh, my goodness! Do you suppose he took it away with him? Oh dear, oh dear. Well, I won't be having him in here again, and that's for sure."

"Trouble is, Mrs L, you just can't trust some people. Listen, though. I've got a pal on the market down the Oxpens. I can pick up a decent carving set from him for next to nothing. I'll have a word with him next week."

"Would you, Mr Rudd? That'd be so kind."

"Yep. You just leave it with me."

And Jerry Rudd would prove as good as his word. *"That lodger of mine, Mr Rudd, I don't know what he does for a living, but you'd be hard pushed to find a nicer or kinder gentleman anywhere. And always so busy..."* (Even though he'd been short-changing her on the rent for as long as he'd lodged there, as well as fleecing the poor woman over everything else. And busy? Alright – but not in doing any honest work...)

Yes, that all summed up Jerry Rudd most eloquently.

Walking with his usual swagger, he headed down the street to the telephone kiosk. It was a pity Mrs Lynch didn't have a phone, because it would have saved Jerry a lot of money. Still, she'd left a whole pile of pennies lying around on the sideboard, and most of those were now jingling merrily in Jerry's trouser pocket.

Once in the kiosk, he was soon through to the number he wanted. A hesitant voice answered. "Yes? Who's calling?"

"Hello there, squire. Remember me, do you?"

"You! Why are you calling me again?"

"Because we're due for a little chat, you and me."

"I've already given you what you wanted. I thought we'd agreed that was it, that you wouldn't call anymore..."

Jerry's voice cut in, shedding its veneer of mateyness. "I don't reckon I'd agreed to anything, squire."

"You did! That information I gave you. You said you could use it, promised to leave me alone."

"Oh, I did, did I? Well, sadly, plans have changed. See, that little venture's not turning out as well as we'd hoped. I got in touch with her the other night, and the silly mare went all hysterical. She's pleading poverty, 'cause she's cleared out her savings and now she's scared stiff her hubby's going to start asking awkward questions. If we're not careful, she might get desperate enough to call in the old Bill. And we wouldn't want that, would we? In short, squire, this ain't turning out to be much of an earner."

"Well, that's hardly my fault," snapped the affronted voice on the other end of the line. "I've done everything you've asked of me, and I don't want anything more to do with it, I tell you. If this woman won't co-operate, I'm afraid that's your problem."

Jerry felt himself start to lose patience. The time had come to let this geezer know just how it was going to be. "Alright, squire. Now you listen to me for a moment. We need to meet up, you and me."

"Meet up? Why? I've nothing more to say."

"Oh, but I reckon you might have. See, I think you've got something to hide."

"Me?" A nervous laugh. "You're barking up the wrong tree, *squire*. I've got nothing to hide." But the voice was a giveaway, completely lacking conviction. "I'll have you know I'm an honest citizen in a decent job. And I pay my taxes."

Jerry winced. "Know how to hit a bloke below the belt too, don't you? Listen, don't piss me around. I mean, just don't. I'm the wrong bloke for that. Now, squire, my reckoning is that you've done something you shouldn't have. Something that perhaps the old Bill might be interested in. I mean, just supposing I let slip your name to one of my copper acquaintances? It's my bet they might make something of it. That's why I think we ought to come to some arrangement, you and me. And it's no good you trying to duck out of it, 'cause I'm not the sort of bloke to go away in a hurry. Let's see now. How would you be fixed for us to meet up on Sunday evening?"

Jerry Rudd chuckled as he let the door of the kiosk swing shut and walked back up the street. Putty in his hands. That's what his new best friend was about to become. Oh, he'd whinge and blubber and beg for mercy, and Jerry would cut him some slack, just a bit, so that the miserable geezer would think he was doing him a favour, and what a reasonable bloke he was for a blackmailer. But Jerry had him. There was no doubt in his mind about that. He had him, and he wasn't about to let him go in a hurry.

He decided to call in at The Boat by way of celebration. It wouldn't be busy this time of the evening. He was right. The little snug – Mick had the temerity to call it the lounge bar – was deserted, and the last customer had left his empty scotch glass on the counter. Mick was round in the tap room, burbling away to some crony about yesterday afternoon's wrestling on the telly, so Jerry took the opportunity to nip behind the bar and serve himself a double scotch from the optic. He was back on a stool and had just drained the glass as Mick rumbled along.

"Wotcher, Jerry. How's tricks?"

"Not so bad, Mick. Draw us half of bitter, will you?" That'd see the end of Grandma Lynch's loose change, and it hadn't cost Jerry a penny of his own money. He was on top form.

"Not run into that stable lad recently?" Mick asked, as he thumped Jerry's glass down in front of him.

"Well, yes, as it happens," Jerry lied. "Plumpton, next Sat'day, he reckons. The 2.30. Happy Go Lucky. Can't miss, in his opinion."

"I'll put a few bob on each way, then. Pint in it for you, if it comes in."

"Oh, I reckon it will," said Jerry cheerfully. "'Cause I'm on a roll at the moment. This latest business venture really looks as if it's going my way."

Everything he touched seemed to be turning to gold. Happy Go Lucky – it summed him up.

6

Just as Neal Gallian had settled down with the newspaper and looking forward to a restful Sunday at home, the phone rang. Jill emerged from the kitchen and was first to it, although Neal was quickly on his feet, anticipating the call would be for him.

"He's right here," Jill was saying. "Oh, I'm sure he'll appreciate it…No, I don't think so either." She smiled ruefully as she handed him the receiver. "Sergeant Wrightson," she added for his benefit.

"Morning, Tom. I take it you're calling from the nick?"

"Too right, lad, and sorry for being about to mess up your Sunday, particularly as we'd told the DCI that things were relatively quiet."

"I take it they aren't now."

"'Fraid not. Something urgent's cropped up. I've just had the DCI on the blower. He's not a happy man."

"Sounds like the ACC's on his back?"

"Got it in one. Mr Streatley's been on to the Guv'nor this morning. He's asking for our 'best man' to get out right away to Farway House. Know it?"

"Would that be the local MP's place, out beyond Appleton?"

"Spot on. Mr Dalton Horwood, no less. It seems his daughter's been kidnapped, and while he's been hobnobbing with the ACC, the trail's getting colder. If you ask me, there's something not quite ringing true about it. In Mr Streatley's informed opinion, there's some undesirable boyfriend on the scene, and it might be a put-up job to get hold of some ransom money. Streatley's demanding the utmost discretion and no, repeat *no* publicity, and he wants to be kept up to date. The Guv'nor insisted on handling that part – his way of keeping involved and making sure the ACC doesn't make any rash promises. DI Winter's not due here until tomorrow, but the Guv'nor's adamant he wants you and Dakers out there this morning and fill Winter in on it when he gets here. Dakers is already on her way in."

"Okay, Tom. I'll get down to you right away. We'll go out to Farway House, get the full picture from Mr Horwood and report back to the DCI at the end of the day."

"Knew I could count on you, Neal. See you shortly."

Tom rang off, and Neal replaced the receiver. He was chuffed that Don Pilling was counting on him and Sally Dakers. They'd made a good team since she'd come to them from Banbury eight months previously. However, he'd been looking forward to a Sunday off and guessed Sally had, too: she'd said something about going home to spend the day with her parents. He also noted the DCI's intention to keep Phil Winter out of the loop for as long as possible: his way of showing the ACC that he was still the man in charge.

Jill had already slipped into her coat and shoes, having rightly guessed the drift of Neal's conversation. "I'll run you down there, darling," she offered cheerfully.

"Jill, I'm really sorry about this."

"It can't be helped. I married a police detective with my eyes wide open, and I haven't regretted it yet. Will it be okay if I prepare dinner for seven o'clock?"

The clock on the mantelpiece showed nine-fifteen. "I certainly hope so," Neal sighed.

*

The unmarked dark blue police Anglia was as official as Neal intended to look, as Sally Dakers drove them out to Farway House. As they came in sight of the open wrought-iron gates, Neal noticed that the grass outside the high drystone wall looked badly churned up, an appearance not in keeping with the glistening lawns either side of the long, gravelled drive. He imagined the garden parties held there during the summer, the house as its backdrop, imposing with its white façade, balconies and high sash windows. Beyond it stood a neat row of stables and outhouses, and he guessed the grounds at the rear of the house would boast a croquet lawn and open-air swimming pool.

A man was waiting beneath the porch as they drew up, and Neal immediately recognized him from a plethora of photographs in the local press, featuring him at various functions in and around Oxford. He looked close to fifty, of medium height, stocky and businesslike, with receding dark hair, a toothbrush moustache and haughty expression. He wore a brown tweed jacket and plus fours, very much in a lord of the manor mode. Neal hoped first impressions would prove wrong. Often, they didn't.

The man strode forward as they got out of the car, and the movement allowed Neal a glimpse of the woman standing behind him some way back from the door. As she followed her husband towards them, Neal put her at a few years younger and around the same height. She appeared a little dowdy in a Cashmere cardigan and calf-length pleated grey skirt. Her russet-coloured hair looked tangled, and she wore no make-up to relieve her pale features. However, she advanced upon them with a pleasant smile, which was more than they were getting from her husband.

He wasn't standing on ceremony, flinging out a brisk hand, which Neal shook a little dazedly. "Good morning, Chief Inspector Pilling. I'm Dalton Horwood."

Neal was alert to Sally Dakers' controlled smirk. "I'm Detective Sergeant Gallian, sir," he corrected politely. "And this is WDC Dakers."

Horwood ignored Sally and glared at Neal. "I'd specifically asked Clive Streatley…" he began.

Neal held up a placatory hand. "There's no-one more senior available at present, I'm afraid, Mr Horwood. DCI Pilling's incapacitated with an ankle injury, and his temporary replacement isn't due down from London until tomorrow."

Horwood threw up his hands in a theatrical gesture. "Heavens, what a shambles! I expected better than this. I take it you know who I am?"

"We're in no doubt about that, sir. But we felt you'd appreciate WDC Dakers and I getting the investigation up and running as quickly as possible."

"I see. Well, it'll have to do, won't it? But I intend letting Streatley know that I'm far from happy."

His wife stepped out of the shadow of the doorway. "Dalton, I really think we should allow these officers to go about their work. After all, our daughter has been abducted." Neal was aware of the edge to her quietly spoken words. It was his first proper view of her, and he observed that she was still a pretty woman, despite her strained expression and the sheen of recent tears on her cheeks.

"Eh? Oh, very well, Marjorie." The MP seemed to notice Dakers for the first time and stared at her accusingly. "Huh! You're a woman."

Marjorie Horwood sighed and looked away, while Sally replied innocuously, "That's right, Mr Horwood."

"Are there such things as women detectives? What *is* the world coming to? Ah well, I suppose we have to make do with you."

Horwood strode off, and they followed him inside, his wife consoling Sally with a smile. Although Neal knew she'd hardly need consoling. The MP's comment might have made most people feel about two inches high, but one thing he liked about Sally Dakers was that whatever she might be feeling inside, she always managed to present a brave face in adversity of any kind. Neal noticed, too, that Sally, despite wearing flat shoes, was still several inches taller than Dalton Horwood. There, he suspected, might lie the rub.

Horwood took them into a spacious, square hallway, lined with light oak panelling, where several doors led off to other parts of the house and a wide, carpeted stairway curved away to the upper floors, a succession of watercolour prints of country scenes lining the walls. Neal suspected Marjorie Horwood's hand in that, and no doubt in several of the other rooms.

A set of double doors stood open across the hallway, but before he took them into the room, the MP turned and addressed them, his manner imperious.

"Our daughter Cressida has been abducted," he announced, not bothering to keep his voice down. "She and the young man accompanying her were supposedly set upon outside my gates in the early hours of this morning. I'm certain a ransom note will shortly follow, but in my opinion the person behind it all is skulking in this room."

"Oh, Dalton, you can't *possibly* know that," Marjorie Horwood protested.

"Well, we're about to find out, aren't we?" Horwood turned smartly on his heel and led them into the room, where a disconsolate young man sat hunched in an armchair beside the fireplace. Two chesterfields and a second armchair were gathered round the roaring fire, and Horwood indicated for the detectives to take one. Neal did so, while Sally stood behind him, her notebook at the ready. Marjorie seemed to dither in the doorway, then, making up her mind, marched across the room to stand defiantly beside the young man and stare reproachfully at her husband.

The MP went and stood before the fire, fixed the huddled figure with a hard stare and flung out a hand towards him. "I think, Sergeant," he proclaimed, "that you'll find this to be your man."

The figure, a bandage round his head and sticking plaster on his chin, looked up wearily. "As I keep saying, Mr Horwood," he said levelly, "it was nothing to do with me. I was the one they attacked."

"As anyone with eyes can see," Marjorie grumbled. "Dalton, you could at least hear him out."

The appeal left her husband looking unmoved. "Right, Nolan," he barked. "These people are police officers, and they've come to hear you confess. Tell them where your cohorts have taken my daughter."

"I've nothing to confess," the young man declared doggedly. "I tried to rescue Cress, and they knocked me unconscious." He looked over at Neal and Sally. "That's the honest truth, but he won't believe me. I don't know who's taken her, but I want her back as much as he does, if not more." His voice broke on the last words, and Marjorie Horwood rested a consoling hand on his shoulder. He turned and looked up at her gratefully.

He was in his early twenties and must have begun the previous evening looking very smart. But his blue suit was dappled with mud, his tie askew and the collar of his button-down shirt ripped. His trousers were streaked with mud.

He cut a sorry figure, and Neal quickly interposed, jumping in ahead of Dalton Horwood's next derisory observation.

"Mr Nolan. I'm Detective Sergeant Gallian from Oxford CID, and this is WDC Dakers. First of all, we need your full name and address."

"My name's Dennis Nolan," the boy replied. He gave an address in Blackhall Road, Oxford, just off St Giles.

Neal watched him as he was speaking, observing the state he was in, the injuries he'd sustained. He felt that if Nolan had had anything at all to do with Cressida Horwood's abduction, he'd certainly suffered for it.

And he couldn't help wondering if the case they were embarking upon would prove to be quite as straightforward as their local MP might think.

7

Neal could tell that Dennis Nolan was unsettled by Dalton Horwood's inimical presence, but it was partly counterbalanced by Marjorie's supportive nearness. The boy focused his attention on the two detectives, and Neal sensed Sally's encouraging smile, aware that she'd slightly shifted her position, so that Nolan wouldn't have the MP obstructing the corner of his vision.

Nolan spoke politely, his voice tinged with a homely Oxfordshire accent, and he came across as a decent enough young man. Clearly, Horwood's main objection was the age-old one of class: he'd move heaven and earth to ensure that his daughter didn't commit the unforgivable sin of marrying beneath her.

"I picked Cress up from here at about seven, and we drove into Oxford, parked round by my pad. A band was playing in the Silver Horseshoe in St Giles: the Rhythmetics – a friend of mine's the lead singer." He gave the boy's name, which Sally noted down. "The performance must have finished around ten."

"So, how do you account for your whereabouts between ten and midnight?" Horwood barked, so suddenly that Nolan started. Marjorie, beside his chair, darted a look of annoyance at her husband.

Neal said, much more quietly, "Mr Nolan?" and reclaimed the boy's attention.

"Oh, er, we went back to my pad in Blackhall Road. We were there for well over an hour, playing LPs. I'm into music, Sergeant. I play and sing with my own group, the Magic Cartwheel."

"Huh." The disgruntled mumble came from the direction of the mantelpiece. "They're a load of long-haired layabouts, who all want to be like these wretched Beatle people. I'd bring back National Service, shake up the whole boiling of 'em."

Putting aside his current dishevelled appearance, Neal felt that Dennis Nolan looked smart enough, dressed in the modern way in what would have begun the previous evening as a suit, collar and tie. His sandy hair, curling up just below the ears and a fringe flopping over his forehead, might have been long compared to the traditional short-back-and-sides, but the boy didn't merit Horwood's generic description, and Neal was yet to see where the 'undesirable' tag came in.

He nodded for Nolan to continue, and the boy seemed to take heart from that, a note of enthusiasm creeping into his voice.

"I also strummed along to some of my own compositions. You see, the group's cutting a demo disc next month, and I wanted Cress's opinion on some of the lyrics I'd written."

"Oh, for heaven's sake, her name is *Cressida*," Horwood growled, possibly to himself, because no-one paid him any attention.

"Other than that, we drank some coffee, smoked a couple of cigarettes and then it was time to drive back here."

"Two hours later than I'd instructed her, *and* she's smoking against my express wishes."

This was rich coming from Horwood, Neal thought, noting a clutch of pipes in a jar on the mantelpiece as well as a silver cigarette case and ashtray on the coffee table. He doubted that both belonged to Marjorie.

"Cigarettes?" he asked lightly.

The boy took the question in the spirit it was intended, with the ghost of a smile. "Not joints, I assure you, Sergeant. We're not into anything like that."

A rumble of disgust came from the expected direction, and Neal guessed Dennis Nolan was quietly enjoying this gentle winding-up of the MP.

"On the way back here," he went on, "we discussed the Magic Cartwheel's show at the Horseshoe in a couple of weeks. Cress and our bass guitarist's girlfriend are going to be our backing singers…"

"Huh!"

"She was very excited about that. We had Radio Luxembourg blasting out from my transistor, and the two of us were chorusing along with the numbers. We seemed to reach here in no time. I slowed down, turned off the road and got out to open the gates. That's when it happened.

"I suppose they must have been lurking in the shadow of the wall, because suddenly I was aware of movement and two dark shapes, and they were on me before I could turn round. One of them pinned my arms to my sides, but I managed to swivel round and kick out at the other chap when he came at me."

"I realize that it was dark, and everything happened quickly," Neal said. "But did you notice anything about them?"

"They both wore Mickey Mouse masks. I managed to wriggle out of the first one's grasp, but then the one I'd kicked hit me in the face, and I went down. The other one aimed a kick at me, but I rolled clear and scrambled to my feet, just as Cress was getting out of the car. I tried to stall them, so that she could run off down the drive, but one of them grabbed her and put his hand over her mouth to stop her crying out. The other coshed me from behind, and my head just seemed to explode. The next I knew, I was grovelling around on the grass outside the gates, wondering where I was and what had happened."

"You can't remember seeing anything else – hearing anything? Their voices – something they might have said – a car?"

"Everything was a blur, and neither of them spoke. They took my car – I'd left my keys in the ignition and the engine running when I'd got out to open the gates. I didn't hear anything from Cress – she'd been struggling, and I wonder if they'd done something to keep her quiet. There was the sound of another vehicle driving off. I think they must have left it some way down the road."

"And there were just the two of them? No-one else?"

"I didn't see anyone else, and I was barely conscious. Didn't even see which direction they'd taken, and my head felt like it was bursting. It seemed to take a long time for me to get to my feet. Then I staggered down the drive and hammered on the door. Eventually, Mr Horwood answered it, and I fell inside. I think I must have fainted then, because when I came round, I was sitting in this chair."

"Who patched you up?"

"I did," Marjorie replied, "while Dalton went down to the gates, but of course they were long gone."

Neal acknowledged her with a nod, realizing that it had been a daft question, because he couldn't envisage her husband tending the injured boy. There didn't seem to be any live-in staff, and he assumed any extra help would come in from one of the nearby villages.

"Who knew that you and Miss Horwood would be in Oxford last night?" he asked Nolan.

"Cress might have told a couple of her girlfriends."

"I can give you some names, Sergeant," Marjorie cut in helpfully. "There are two she's very friendly with."

"And Finlay was with us last night," Dennis added.

"Who's he?"

"The son of the farmer at Woodview Farm, a mile down the road. Finlay Cleave. We met at school in Oxford, and we've been friends ever since. Fin's a member of the group. In fact, he introduced me to Cress."

Neal switched a glance towards Dalton Horwood. There'd been no further interruptions from him, but his tortured expression told Neal that he was having a battle to hold his tongue.

Neal advised Dennis that he'd have further questions for him before long. He asked for his car details – it was a ten-year-old Austin A30, which Sally noted down – before turning to Horwood to request the use of a telephone.

"Out in the hallway," was the grudging response, and Neal thanked him and sent Sally out to call through to the station, so that patrols and beat officers could keep a lookout for the car.

He further advised Nolan to get himself checked out by a doctor, and Marjorie readily volunteered to run him back home and call in on her doctor on the way, so that the extent of his injuries could be assessed.

"And once you're home, Mr Nolan," Neal added, "I'd be obliged if you'd remain there until you hear either from WDC Dakers or myself."

The boy looked on edge. "Am I – under suspicion?" He cast an involuntary glance at the MP's looming figure, certain that in Horwood's eyes he wasn't just under suspicion but already arrested, tried and convicted.

"At the start of an investigation, everyone is," Neal replied, deliberately allowing his gaze to rest momentarily on Horwood.

"Humph!" The MP watched unimpressed as Marjorie helped Dennis out of his chair. He still seemed shaken, but as he left the room had the good manners to thank Horwood. *What for?* Neal wondered, as he nodded his own goodbye to the young man. And he felt Dennis had acted out of politeness rather than from any other motive.

He heard Sally Dakers, her phone call completed, talking to them in the hallway on their way out, reassuring Nolan that they'd be looking out for his car, which, if they had any sense, the kidnappers would by now have abandoned somewhere.

As he was getting to his feet, Dalton Horwood approached him. He nodded towards the window, past which his wife and Dennis Nolan were walking on their way round to where the cars were garaged. A few minutes later, they drove away in a new-looking Land Rover.

"An unnecessary fuss, if you ask me," Horwood grumbled. "But Marjorie will coddle the boy, as she does with Cressida. Well, Sergeant?"

"Well, sir, the only lead we have at present is Mr Nolan's car. Once we've found that, we can make inquiries as to whether anyone in the vicinity may have noticed anything. We'll ask around your daughter's and Mr Nolan's friends and see if they can throw any light on the matter. I agree that it may well all hang on the appearance of a ransom demand. Please get in touch with us as soon as the kidnappers make contact, but don't do anything until we've advised you."

Horwood nodded his understanding. "I don't want any of this to get out," he said firmly. "ACC Streatley assured me the matter would be handled with the utmost discretion."

"We'll not be giving out any details, sir," Neal replied. "Sadly, the press have their peculiar ways of turning up information, and your position as an MP would make it a very newsworthy story."

Horwood allowed himself a satisfied little smile at that, but his voice was stern. "That mustn't happen."

"I agree. If anyone asks after your daughter, it'd probably be best if you told them she was away visiting a relative. We shall make sure anyone we interview understands the delicate nature of the situation."

"I'm obliged," Horwood replied, as he accompanied Neal out to the hallway, where Sally was waiting, and saw them to the door.

"Sergeant, I apologize for my earlier outburst," he went on. "Cressida is very precious to myself and Marjorie. She's our only child and, sadly, used to getting her own way. I don't approve of her relationship with Nolan, but she's rather headstrong and insists that she wants to marry him. I refuse to contemplate it. The boy works in a record store and has ambitions to be a pop singer, if ever you did, and I certainly won't have a daughter of mine marrying beneath her class.

"My worry is that this abduction may be something they've cooked up between them. Perhaps I shouldn't think it of Cressida, but I'm afraid she'd be capable of it. Oh, I accept that the boy's injuries are real, but maybe his so-called attacker was simply over-zealous in an attempt to make things look realistic. However, time will tell. Inform your superior that I shall be in touch the moment I hear from the kidnappers."

"Thank you, sir. I'll report to DI Winter in the morning. I'm sure he'll get in touch with you as a matter of urgency."

Horwood nodded his thanks and held open the door. He'd already closed it by the time they'd reached the car.

"Honestly, Sarge," Sally remarked as they drove down towards the gates, "you should get a medal for patience. You must have felt like punching his lights out."

"Certainly not, WDC Dakers." Neal sounded indignant. "Whatever gave you that impression? I doubt if the man has a biased bone in his body."

They held back their laughter until they'd driven beyond the gates.

8

However, once they'd turned out on to the road, Neal told Sally to pull the car into the side, so that they could have a look at the spot where Dennis Nolan had been attacked. As he'd expected, they found nothing to help them. There were obvious signs of a scuffle where the grass had been churned up, but nothing in the way of footprints, and no tell-tale items which the kidnappers had been careless enough to drop. A hundred yards or so in either direction was a passing-place, and Neal guessed that the kidnappers had parked their own car in one of them. Dennis Nolan had said he'd heard a second vehicle moving off. He decided to send a couple of uniforms out to go over the ground again but felt certain they'd find no clues. Although at least he believed it should satisfy Horwood that they weren't dragging their heels in their efforts to find his daughter.

Woodview Farm, where Nolan's friend Finlay Cleave lived, was only a mile further on, so they took the opportunity to call on him before returning to Oxford.

A shooting brake and Ford Prefect stood in the yard outside the solidly built stone farmhouse, whose door was opened by a round, rosy-cheeked woman of fifty. Showing his warrant card, Neal stated the purpose of their visit, and the woman's face clouded slightly. "He's not in trouble, I hope?" she asked.

"Not at all, Mrs Cleave," Neal replied. "It's just that he may be able to help us with an aspect of the investigation we're working on."

"Come on in, then, both of you, and take a seat. I dare say you could use a nice, hot cup of tea on this chilly morning?"

They thanked her, and she filled the kettle and put it on the Aga. "I'll go and fetch him," Mrs Cleave went on. "He's still in bed. Got home late last night. He'd been in Oxford seeing his young lady – they'd been to some pop concert, I think he said."

Neal and Sally took chairs round the long kitchen table, savouring the aroma of the joint roasting in the oven. He was reminded that he and Jill should shortly have been sitting down to their Sunday lunch and resolved to wind things up for the day as soon as he decently could, so that he might get back home and spend the remainder of the afternoon and evening with her.

Moments later, Finlay Cleave tumbled in, a stocky lad with ruddy cheeks like his mother and a shock of fair hair. He looked like he'd thrown on his clothes in a hurry, his shirt tail hanging outside his rumpled jeans. Mrs Cleave, still smiling, followed him in and made and poured them all a mug of tea before diplomatically leaving the room.

Finlay looked apprehensive, and Neal, pointing him to a seat, decided to quickly set the boy's mind at rest.

"Mr Cleave, we're here to ask if you were with Dennis Nolan and Cressida Horwood yesterday evening?"

"Why, yes," the boy answered readily. "We were at the Silver Horseshoe in St Giles, listening to this group. A couple of the members are friends of ours." He frowned anxiously. "What's this about? Is everything alright?"

Neal wasn't ready to answer that question yet. "What time did they leave?"

"Just after ten, when the session finished. They were going to Denny's pad, which isn't far away."

"You didn't go with them?"

"No, I was with my girlfriend, Bella Sims. She lives down the Abingdon Road, and I drove her home."

"Did you come straight back here afterwards?" Neal felt it unlikely that Finlay Cleave had been involved in the assault and kidnapping, but the question had to be asked.

The boy grinned. "Not for a while. She shares a house with two other girls, and we all sat round drinking coffee and playing records. It went on a bit long, and a neighbour came round and hammered on the door, telling us to put a sock in it. I stayed with Bella a while longer, must have come away about one o'clock and drove home."

Sally Dakers cut in to ask Bella's address and the names of her housemates, noting down the details.

"And your car's out in the yard, Mr Cleave?" Neal asked.

"The Prefect? Yes, that's mine. Sergeant, what's this about? Are Denny and Cress okay?"

Neal had known from the moment Dalton Horwood had made the request that it wasn't going to be possible to keep this under wraps. He exchanged a glance with Sally, sensing they were on the same wavelength.

"Miss Horwood and Mr Nolan were assaulted last night at the gates of Farway House," he said. "The attackers took Miss Horwood off in Mr Nolan's car."

Finlay looked stunned. "Cress has been – *kidnapped?*"

"It looks that way."

"And what about Denny? Is he okay?"

"He suffered a blow to the head as well as some cuts and bruises. Mrs Horwood has taken him to see her doctor before driving him home."

"Is it okay for me to phone him?"

"Perhaps later this afternoon. Listen, Mr Cleave. We hope to clear this up quickly and ensure Miss Horwood's safety. You'll know that her father's an MP, and as such he doesn't want the press to get hold of this. Everything I've told you is in confidence. I don't want you to tell anyone about it – as in anyone at all. Do you understand that?"

"Yes, yes, I do. Denny and Cress are real good friends of mine. I'll do whatever I can to help."

"That's good. Now, have you any idea who might be behind this?"

Finlay shrugged helplessly. "None at all."

"You're in a pop group with Mr Nolan, aren't you?"

"Yes, the Magic Cartwheel."

"Any rivalries at all within the group? Anyone outside it who might begrudge your success?"

"No, we're all good mates – four lads who were at secondary school together. As for success, well, we haven't really had any. We're a decent band, like so many others locally. And okay, we're cutting a demo next month, but that doesn't guarantee anything at all."

Neal decided to leave it there, at least for the time being. He asked Finlay again to keep to himself what he'd just learned, adding that they'd be in touch again before long. "Better tell your mother we were asking about some incident – a fight, perhaps – that happened in Oxford last night, and if you'd witnessed it," he added, grinning. "Oh - and assure her we're not likely to be placing you under arrest."

Back in the car, Neal told Sally to head for Oxford. He asked her to drop in on Cressida's two friends, whose addresses Marjorie Horwood had given them, as well as Finlay's girlfriend, Bella Sims. She could take the car, having first dropped him off in Blackhall Road to call in on Dennis Nolan. They agreed that Finlay Cleave seemed to check out and were fairly certain Cressida's friends would do the same.

"Then leave the car at the nick and the keys at the desk and go home. Sorry that this has wrecked your day off."

Sally shrugged stoically. "I phoned Mum and Dad this morning, before I left my digs. They understand, and we've agreed to meet up next Sunday instead."

Several of the Victorian terraced houses in the area behind St Giles had been turned into flats. Dennis Nolan's was a large basement room, smelling a little damp, its walls lined with posters of pop artists and groups. The furniture looked ancient and cumbersome, and the Baby Belling cooker had seen better days. There was bound to be a shared bathroom and kitchen somewhere in the rambling house. The focus of the room was the Dansette record player, every surface around it covered with LP sleeves: Kinks, Searchers, Hollies and Manfred Mann, as well as back numbers of New Musical Express and Melody Maker. An electric guitar and a small keyboard stood eloquently in a corner. It was a typical young person's pad, particularly one who was so deeply into pop music, several worlds removed from the idea of the young man Dalton Horwood would wish for his daughter.

Marjorie's doctor had applied a fresh bandage round Dennis's forehead, and he told Neal he'd been prescribed a bottle of painkillers and told to rest up for a couple of days, when he'd check him over again. Neal was glad to see him looking somewhat better than he had that morning but guessed that he wouldn't be able to settle to anything until they had news of Cressida.

"I just wanted to see you somewhere other than Farway House," he explained, "and I'm sure you'll give me an honest answer. But in your opinion, is the kidnapping something Cressida might be capable of dreaming up?"

Dennis thought about it for a moment, a smile playing on his lips. "Cress can be wilful," he answered at last. "Her parents dote on her – Mrs Horwood's a lovely, caring person – but she and her father don't always see eye to eye. I know he dislikes me, because he feels I'm beneath his class. But Cress and I are very much in love. We've been seeing one another for well over a year, and there's no way she'd let anyone do to me what they did. And from what little I witnessed last night – no, Cress couldn't have faked that. The abduction was for real, and she certainly had no hand in it."

Neal nodded his acceptance of Dennis's explanation. "I've spoken to Finlay Cleave," he went on. "He's concerned about you and said he'd give you a ring."

"He already has," Dennis replied and added, as he saw Neal casting about for a phone, "There's a pay phone behind the door up on the landing. Fin always calls me there."

"He'll have told you about our chat, then?"

"He did. Fin's a good friend, Sergeant Gallian. In fact, all of us in the band get on well, and I assure you none of them would be into something as heavy as this. We're aiming to secure a recording contract for Cartwheel, because we all want to move on from our low-paid jobs. No-one in the band would want to jeopardize our future."

Neal thanked Dennis for what he believed were candid views and said he'd be in touch. He was coming round to believe the kidnapping had been for real, and that it wouldn't be long before the miscreants made contact with Dalton Horwood. He asked Dennis to be patient until then. If he heard or remembered anything else, he was to get in touch with Neal or

Sally Dakers right away. He added that they'd be in touch with Dennis as soon as they had some news about his car.

He called in at the station before catching a bus home. Tom Wrightson hadn't heard anything about the car, but DCI Pilling had phoned in to request an update. Neal went along to his office to return the call.

"Rather glad it's you and not me on this one, Neal," Pilling commented, once Neal had given his report. "I'd have had to bite my tongue to prevent myself putting our esteemed MP in his place. Okay, call it a day now. I'm sorry that it's ruined a day off for you and Dakers, but as you know, that's police work. You'd better get in early tomorrow to report to DI Winter. He'll no doubt want to run the investigation, and I'm sure you'll agree he's more than welcome to the Right Honourable Dalton Horwood."

Having said goodbye to Tom, Neal headed home to a welcome from Jill, who hadn't expected him back until later. She put the roast in the oven right away, and he was soon savouring an aroma reminiscent of that in Mrs Cleave's kitchen several hours earlier. Once they'd eaten and cleared away, they settled down to a quiet evening of television.

"I expect you'll need to be down at the station early?" Jill inquired, once the programme they'd been watching had finished.

Neal caught the hint of speculation in her voice. "Yes," he replied. "I'll want to be fresh and alert when I get to meet DI Winter. I'm wondering if we ought to have an early night?"

"Funny, but I was thinking the same," Jill replied.

9

He was down at the station by eight the next morning to find Tom at the front desk, a post from which he rarely seemed to be absent.

"We've found the lad's car, Gally," Tom reported. "Beat copper called it in last night – discovered it on some waste ground up Cowley Marsh. Abandoned but not damaged. Forensics are checking for prints, and I've sent Hodgson round to collect young Nolan's so's we can eliminate him. Dare say it won't get us far, unless the kidnappers are rank amateurs. We'll get the car back to him once they've been over it." Tom leaned forward, lowering his voice. "He's here, Gally, bright and early. Busy rearranging the DCI's office – the Guv'nor'll go up the wall. You'd p'raps best go along and make yourself known."

Neal passed DC Mal Brady and WPC Yvonne Begley in the corridor. They snapped out of their conspiratorial huddle to acknowledge him. Both looked glum.

He'd never met Phil Winter, but Tom had given him some idea of what to expect. Winter was Cambridge-educated and had been stationed at Oxford during the period of Neal's absence. He and the DCI hadn't hit it off. Pilling was old school and not keen on people with university educations. In his opinion such qualifications were superfluous, as you didn't need one to become a good copper. And besides, Winter often hadn't been thorough enough for him, too eager to cut corners and tending to look down on those beneath him in the pecking order. He'd alienated Brady, Yvonne and Pam Harding among others, expecting them always to be at his beck and call.

"The Guv'nor reckoned him too flashy," Tom had said. "Gave CID a bad name. A couple of cases failed to come to court through Winter's oversights, although he tried to lay the blame elsewhere, and on t'other side of the coin, he was quick to claim credit for any success, conveniently forgetting that it had been the lower ranks who'd done all the donkey work. As you'd guess, the ACC liked him – knew Winter's father, as it happened. Helped give him a leg up to DI, and once there our Philip moved swiftly on."

Neal knocked on what, for him, would never be anything other than the DCI's door.

"Come!"

He came. "DI Winter? I'm DS Gallian."

"Ah, yes. Come in." Winter leapt up from his seat, and in two strides was beside Neal and offering a firm hand. They shook, and he pointed Neal to a seat before going to the door and looking out along the corridor.

"Oh, Brady?" Neal heard him say. "Nip along and fetch us two teas, will you?"

Neal stifled a grin at the image of Mal as tea-boy, a task he was always eager to inflict on new recruits. He guessed it wouldn't take his temporary boss long to put his stamp on proceedings. Whether or not that would be a good thing remained to be seen.

Returning to the desk, Winter resumed his seat and grinned across at Neal, each of them briefly summing up the other.

Phil Winter was thirty years old, a little younger than Neal and an inch or so taller. His brown hair was worn traditionally short, and his moustache and correct bearing made Neal wonder if at some time he'd had army officer training. He had an educated, slightly superior voice and looked smart in a light-grey check suit, white shirt, blue tie and gleaming brown brogues. Neal noted the clear desk, which had always been the opposite of clear with Don Pilling behind it. In fact, what looked suspiciously like the DCI's perpetual mountain of paperwork sat on top of the filing cabinet behind Winter, and Neal suspected a certain pipe and Bondman tin might be lurking there too.

Winter had learned of the incident in which Neal had been badly wounded and Clyde Holt killed when he'd first been appointed to Oxford and had the decency to ask if he'd made a full recovery and to add that he was glad he'd returned to the force.

Neal replied positively. He'd been back in the job for almost a year, trying to put the past firmly behind him, and he was glad when Winter left it at that. Once they'd been through the preliminaries, they talked about the case in hand. Don Pilling had phoned Winter the previous day to tell him to expect a full briefing from his DS.

"Please call me Phil, by the way, and I'll try to persuade Uncle Tom to do the same, although he's a stickler for protocol, as you know. I shall be relying on the pair of you to keep me up to date with what's happening. The kidnapping of Dalton Horwood's daughter must be given top priority. So, I'd be grateful for the details of your inquiries to date and your thoughts on where we're going with it."

Neal did so, interrupted only by a subdued Mal Brady, bearing a tray of tea and biscuits. His tie was properly fastened for once, and Neal learned later that Winter's first action on arrival had been to give him a dressing-down over his slovenly appearance. Don Pilling, hardly a picture of sartorial elegance himself, had been inclined to tolerate Brady's habitual scruffiness, but Mal might have known he wasn't going to get away with it where Phil Winter was concerned.

As soon as Brady had left, the tea consumed, and Neal had given the DI chapter and verse on the kidnapping, Winter rang through to the desk and asked for Dakers to be sent in. She arrived and, rather pointedly in Neal's view, wasn't invited to sit.

"Ah, Dakers. Good to meet you. DI Winter. Now, DS Gallian tells me you interviewed Miss Horwood's friends and Finlay Cleave's girlfriend yesterday afternoon?"

It transpired there was nothing to report, and Sally had succeeded in not mentioning anything to the girls about the kidnapping. They worked as secretaries or typists, and Sally felt it unlikely that any of them could be involved.

Winter seemed satisfied with her report and the clear, concise way she'd delivered it. "Good show, Dakers. Discretion's the name of the game, after all. Right, I'd better head out to Farway House and see how the land lies. Perhaps you'd accompany me, Neal?"

They were interrupted by a knock on the door.

"Come!"

Tom Wrightson looked in, formal and stony-faced. "A report's just come in about the discovery of a body close to Walton Well Bridge in

Jericho, sir. I've sent Hodgson down to keep any nosy parkers at bay, and Doc Mather's on his way there now."

"Right. Thanks, Tom." Winter waited for Tom to withdraw and turned to Neal.

"This puts a different complexion on the morning, Sergeant. So, we'd better divide our labours. I'll go out to Farway House. Dakers, you'll be with me. You were out there yesterday too, so you can talk me through your impressions on the drive out. Neal, you'd better get down to Jericho and start investigating what's happened there. You can take Brady with you."

Neal clocked Sally's disappointment in the helpless look she threw him, which the DI didn't notice. They made a good team, and Sally had grown in confidence under Neal's direction during the last few months.

However, it had been Winter's call, and Neal couldn't blame him for having made the right one.

10

Neal found Mal Brady taking refuge in the canteen. He told him they'd received a call-out: a body discovered in the canal down by Walton Well Bridge. Brady nodded, got up and trudged along unhappily in his wake.

At the front desk, Tom Wrightson was looking grim, head bent over some paperwork, while WPCs Yvonne Begley and Pam Harding were having a moan.

"Who does he think he is? Getting Sally to drive him in the Wolseley, if ever you did!"

"Bet he'll sit in the back, trying to look important."

"Well, I shouldn't think Sally 'ud want him in the front with her."

"Oh, I don't think he'd be like that, would he?"

"What? D'you reckon he's one of them, then?"

Tom rapped his knuckles authoritatively on the desk. "Come along now, girls. Enough of this. Let's grit our teeth and show DI Winter what we're capable of. You know DCI Pilling. Rest assured his mishap won't keep him away for long."

Yvonne sighed. "Let's hope not. This morning's had me even feeling sorry for you, DC Brady."

As the WPCs dispersed about their business, Neal explained to Tom where he and Mal were going and led the way out to the yard, with his new sidekick trailing morosely behind him.

"Cheer up, Mal. It may never happen."

"Winter was a bossy sod when he was here before," Brady grunted. "Give me the DCI any day. Well, Gally, looks like you're going to be saddled with me."

"Just do the job we both know you can do, Mal, and we shan't quarrel."

"Suits me."

It was a dull day, with the weak November sun ineffectually trying to pierce the gloom. As they parked the car and walked across Walton Well Bridge, they saw that access to the towpath had been taped off and a familiar white tent set up behind it. Paul Hodgson stood behind the tape, in the act of moving on a small group of would-be sightseers.

He greeted Neal and Brady. "A bloke walking his dog found him about an hour ago, Gally. Think you'll recognize him. The doc's in the tent with him now."

Hubert Mather loomed out of the opening at their approach. He was a tall, gloomy man of few words. "Ah, DS Gallian."

"Morning, Doc. What have you got for us?"

"Come and take a look. Your young PC's confident you'll know him."

Neal ducked inside the tent with Mal at his shoulder. It was cramped for space inside, with the three of them, and the corpse laid out on a ground sheet. Before he'd had his first proper glimpse, Neal knew who it was. The Tyrolean hat over in the corner was identification enough.

Jerry Rudd.

"Drowned?" Neal inquired.

"I'd say the water finished him off. But he was knifed before he got pitched into the canal. A very thin blade – no sign of the weapon. I'd guess he went in late last night."

It was claustrophobic in the tent, and Neal was glad to get back outside. Mather promised to send him the pathology report as soon as he was able. "But I doubt it'll be much different from what I've just given you."

"Blimey," Brady exclaimed, once Mather had returned to his task, "where do we begin? Must've had people queueing up to bump him off."

"Agreed, Mal. But we'll start from here." He went over to where Paul Hodgson stood. "Paul, I'll organize some help for you. Once the doc's packed up and gone, make a search of the bridge and towpath for a thin-bladed weapon, then start a door-to-door. Post one of the WPCs on the towpath to make sure passers-by don't go where they shouldn't. Oh, and since news has a habit of travelling fast, it's likely some journalist or other will turn up – Larry Rackham, like as not. Anyone who does should be referred to me. Okay?"

"Will do, Gally."

Neal went back to the car and patched through to the station asking for a couple of WPCs to help with door-to-door inquiries. Before long, Pam Harding showed up with one of her junior colleagues and, once the search along the towpath had been completed and no weapon or anything of interest to them found, Neal set Pam and Paul Hodgson knocking on doors to discover if anyone had seen or heard anything the previous night. Meanwhile, he and Mal Brady went to break the news to Jerry Rudd's landlady. Neal wasn't sure of the exact address, although he knew it wasn't far from the railway station. Mal, however, had been to the house on a previous inquiry and directed Neal to it.

"Landlady's a Mrs Lynch," he said. "I met her the time I called there. A nice old girl, if a mite too trusting. You can imagine how Jerry would have pulled the wool over her eyes."

Mrs Lynch was very upset by the news. "Oh, poor Mr Rudd. I don't know what work he did, but he was always out and about – such a busy man."

"He was certainly that, Mrs Lynch," Neal confirmed. He sat and had a cup of tea with her while Mal, with her permission, made a quick search of Jerry's room.

"Nothing incriminating," he reported, once they'd left the house. "Room was neat and tidy. Several items looked as though they might have been nicked – couldn't imagine Jerry ever stumping up for 'em. Better get someone down here to make a list and check to see if there's a record of anything reported missing. Couldn't find anything written down – no trace of a notebook, diary or anything like that. Must've kept all the details in his head."

"That sounds like Jerry," Neal replied. "Cautious to the last."

Mrs Lynch had informed them that their lodger had gone out late the previous night. "He said he was off down to The Boat, although it must have been very near to closing time when he left."

That was their next port of call. Mick Jenner, the landlord, a slow-moving mountain of a man, a former wrestler according to some of the framed photographs dotted around the bar, told them that Jerry Rudd called in from time to time, never stayed for long and often arrived with a racing tip, on which he'd be quick to claim a commission if the horse or greyhound came in.

"Jerry's always struck me as being a bit dodgy," Mick went on. "Not surprised you lot are interested in him. What's he done?"

"Upset someone," Neal replied. "We fished him out of the canal this morning, down by Walton Well Bridge."

Mick's mouth dropped open. "What? *Dead?*"

Very, Neal didn't say, nodding instead.

"So, somebody topped him?"

"I can't go into details, Mr Jenner. His landlady told us he said he was calling in here last night. It would have been quite late on."

Mick Jenner was already shaking his head. "Always quiet on a Sunday night, Sergeant, and Jerry never came in, I can swear to it. In fact, I haven't seen him since the middle of last week."

Neal decided they'd take a short break while they could and asked Mick if he could rustle up some sandwiches. They were ham and not at all bad, and Mal decided to keep the right side of his sergeant by sticking with a non-alcoholic drink. Neal wondered how many pints of Morrell's he'd have downed had he been on his own.

The Boat wasn't far from the bridge where Jerry Rudd's body had been found and, as he hadn't called into the pub, Neal guessed he'd have arranged a meeting with someone. With Jerry, money was the end result of every equation, and he wondered if the little man might have been indulging in a spot of blackmail. He was sure it wouldn't have been the first time.

Fortified by their snack, they returned to the crime scene. Mal pitched in and helped Pam with the door-to-door inquiries, while Neal sent Paul Hodgson off for a break. Before he went, Hodgson told him that a reporter had been sniffing around and that, as Neal had predicted, it was Larry Rackham.

"In fact," Paul added, as he was on the point of setting off, "he's coming across the bridge now."

Larry Rackham was an untidy, busy little man of thirty-something with a notebook permanently welded to his hand. He was a freelance journalist, often featuring in various city and county newspapers, perpetually on the lookout for the story which would pitch him into the big-time.

"Ah, DS Gallian. Good day to you. I've heard that a body was fished out of the canal around here this morning. I asked your young constable about it, but he was giving nothing away."

"That's because he's following my orders, Mr Rackham."

"Any information you might be able to give me, DS Gallian?" Larry wheedled.

"Apart from the fact that there was indeed a body in the canal, I've nothing to give you, I'm afraid. And there won't be until we've received the pathology report, and the corpse has been formally identified. Sorry about that, Mr Rackham, but it's probably too late for copy now anyway."

"Oh, it's never too late for copy, Sergeant," Larry grinned. "Doors are always springing open somewhere along the line."

"And in any case, I'd have to refer you to DI Winter. He's in temporary charge."

Larry's beaten-up face lit up. "Oh, is he now? I'd heard of Mr Pilling's mishap. Hhmm, I remember DI Winter. Quite a personable young man."

"Well, you'd better give him a call. Doubt if you'll find him in today, as he's out on an inquiry."

"Thank you, DS Gallian. Be assured I'll make contact." The grin stretched wider. "Dare say he'll be a tad more forthcoming than DCI Pilling usually is."

"Don't hold your breath," Neal warned him. Besides, Rackham would have to get past Uncle Tom first.

Once Paul Hodgson had returned, he sent Pam and her colleague off for their break. The search along the towpath had revealed nothing, and so far no information of any use had come from the door-to-door inquiries. Neal worked alongside Brady and Hodgson, making a note of those addresses where there'd been no-one at home so that they could call again later. It was well on into the afternoon when Pam discovered something of interest. Neal went along to join her.

Two residents of one of the small, terraced houses, a young married couple, had been to a cinema the previous evening for a late showing.

"It was about eleven or just after when we got back," the husband said. "And blow me, if there wasn't a car parked outside our house, right where we usually leave ours."

"Another resident?" Neal asked.

The man shook his head. "It wasn't anyone from around here. White car, newish, a Cortina, I think. Well, Sandra and me managed to park further down the street, but as I said to your WPC here, we noticed the car 'cause it had a row of stickers in the back window from Butlin's holiday camps. Filey, Clacton and Pwllheli – which was where we spent our honeymoon last summer."

"Did you notice anything else about it? Was it still there this morning?"

"No, it had gone. And we never heard it drive off."

"Did you get the registration number?"

"Sorry, I'm afraid not."

Neal thanked the couple. It was a possible lead, if a tenuous one and, as things transpired, all they got from a lot of legwork. He called his team together as darkness fell and sent them on their way, setting Mal and

Pam the task for the following day of putting together a list of Jerry Rudd's known associates, tracking them down and interviewing them.

"Should keep us busy till Christmas, Sarge," Pam commented drily.

"Easter," Mal added glumly.

11

As Sally drove away from the station, Phil Winter instructed her to make a short detour before they went out to Farway House. His voice sounded quite distant from where he sat in the back seat of the Wolseley, trying, Sally was sure, to look important.

"Don Pilling's asked me to call in on him," he said. "There are a couple of issues he wants me to clear up."

"Yes, sir."

As they turned on to the Pillings' drive, Winter got out and told Sally to remain where she was, as he didn't expect to be long. But once Sheila Pilling had admitted him, she came back to the door and beckoned for her to come in.

"It's Sally, isn't it? Can't have you waiting out there in the cold. Come into the kitchen, and I'll pour you a cup of tea."

"That's very kind, Mrs Pilling."

"It's Sheila, dear."

They spent a cosy twenty minutes together. Sheila originally hailed from Banbury and was delighted to learn that Sally had grown up there. They chatted away companionably, aware all the while of the DCI's no-nonsense voice issuing from the adjacent room, and Phil Winter's respectful and cautious replies.

"I don't think your new boss is going to be too happy," Sheila whispered. "Because I know Donald isn't – although that's not unusual. Another of those bear-with-sore-head days is brewing."

Once the conversation in the next room seemed to be winding down, Sally thanked Sheila and explained that it would be diplomatic for her to return to the car. Sheila agreed with a nod and rueful smile, and Sally was back behind the wheel when Winter emerged.

"Farway House, Dakers," he instructed crisply.

He sounded a little peeved but seemed restored to equanimity before long, and once Sally had updated him on the investigation so far, he asked her how long she'd been with the police and what she thought of Oxford? She guessed he was digging for information about her colleagues and made sure to be positive about everyone, even Mal Brady.

"Hhmm, yes. I spoke to DS Gallian for the first time this morning. He seems to have his wits about him."

"Yes, sir. I've learned a lot from him," Sally replied, wishing she might add, *perhaps you could too.*

Winter went on to fill her in on his career to date, strangely glossing over his time in Oxford and concentrating on the last year or so with the Met. He focused on a recent operation where a team of detectives had foiled a jewel robbery in Hatton Garden. The way he told it, he'd masterminded the whole investigation, but Sally, while nodding along and trying to look impressed, suspected he'd been merely a junior member of the team.

As they turned off the main road into the winding lanes which led to Farway House, Winter began to warm to the task ahead.

"Dalton Horwood's been the local MP in the last two parliaments," he enthused, "and there's a possibility he'll make the next Conservative cabinet when they're re-elected. We must make sure to keep him on-side, Dakers, and pull out all the stops on this one."

They came in sight of the house. "My stars!" Winter exclaimed. "What a pile!"

In the rear-view mirror, Sally saw him leaning forward to take in his surroundings. His look of awe suggested it might be his ambition to achieve something similar. Perhaps the next ACC? She imagined DCI Pilling's reaction to that: he'd probably resign in high dudgeon, to put it mildly.

A dumpy, smiling woman in a housecoat answered the door to them, and Marjorie Horwood, in a smart grey suit and with hair less tangled than on the previous day, appeared behind her moments later. "Thank you, Mrs Davis. I'll take it from here."

The woman bobbed her head. "Ma'am," she murmured and disappeared into the far reaches of the house, as Winter introduced himself and shook hands with Marjorie. A door opened across the wide hallway, and her husband came out, tweed-jacketed but with dark flannels replacing the plus-fours, which Sally suspected had been his weekend outfit.

He strode across to join them, and Winter stepped past Marjorie to greet him.

"Mr Horwood – a pleasure to meet you, sir. Detective Inspector Philip Winter."

Dalton Horwood's expression was approving. "Good morning, Winter. I must say you seem a cut above what I'd expect of a Detective Inspector. Oxford or Cambridge?"

"Cambridge, sir."

"Ah, good man." He glanced towards his wife. "Marjorie, I think it best if I talk to DI Winter alone. We'll be in the study."

"You can wait here, Dakers," Winter said, suddenly seeming alive to Sally's existence, as he turned and followed the MP.

Marjorie Horwood's lips compressed in a resigned smile. "Honestly, these men! Come along. I can't call you Dakers, you must have another name?"

"It's Sally, madam."

"I know when I'm surplus to requirements, Sally, and I guess you do, too. Let's have some coffee." She picked up a small bell from the hallstand, rang it, and the woman who'd answered the door to them appeared from a room across the hallway. "May we have some coffee, please, Mrs Davis? We'll be in my little sitting room."

Mrs Davis smiled, bobbed her head and returned whence she'd come, while Marjorie led Sally into a pretty little room with armchairs in green brocade, a coffee table, small bookcase, compact radiogram and a worktable containing knitting and embroidery.

"I come here to escape," Marjorie confided. "It's good to have a bolt hole when my husband, his agent and other guests are talking politics. "I -er, take it Detective Inspector Winter is the Chief Inspector's replacement?"

"Only temporarily," Sally corrected her. "Mr Pilling will return as soon as he's able."

"I liked the young man who came here with you yesterday. Detective Sergeant Gallian? He struck me as being sensitive as well as efficient. I should imagine you enjoy working with him?"

"Er, yes, very much." Sally hoped she wasn't blushing but was saved by Mrs Davis' arrival with a tray of coffee and biscuits. She believed that it was more than DI Winter was likely to be getting. Marjorie did the honours, and Sally bit thankfully into a delicious shortbread. She'd been in a hurry that morning and had had to skip breakfast. As Marjorie handed her a coffee, she leaned towards her confidentially.

"Sally, your detective inspector seems a pleasant young man, but I hope he won't allow himself to be led on by my husband. Dalton's a politician through and through, bursting with opinions and always right. He means well, I know, but he's got it into his head that Dennis Nolan is behind the kidnapping of our daughter. The more I think about it, I believe it's for real, not a scheme that's been dreamed up by Cressida and Dennis.

"Despite what Dalton might say, Dennis Nolan's a nice boy, and Cressida's calmed down a lot since they met. I'm able to see, if Dalton can't or won't, that they have a genuine affection for one another, and I'm convinced that Dennis would never do anything to harm or cause her pain – and a woman notices these things, my dear."

It was a plea from the heart, but Sally saw the opportunity to probe further and felt she had to take it.

"I hope you won't be offended, Mrs Horwood, but we do have to explore the possibility that Cressida and Dennis planned the abduction between them for the ransom money."

"No offence taken, Sally," Marjorie smiled back. "But Dennis's injuries were for real – I know because I tended them, and I also know Cressida would never have let him suffer like that. Dalton would wish the boy to be guilty simply because he feels he's beneath us."

"And you'd count out their friends?"

"I'd believe it nigh on impossible for any of Cressida's girlfriends to be involved in anything like this. Otherwise, the only one of their joint friends I know is Finlay Cleave. He's an open and honest young man, and I like his parents. Also, there seems to be no friction between Dennis, Finlay and the other boys in their group. I'm afraid that sometimes my husband can be too quick to point the finger." Marjorie paused, grimacing. "Sometimes, I'm sure Cressida rebels just to spite her father. Oh, never in the way we've just mentioned – nothing as drastic as that," she added quickly. "Dalton's been threatening to send her to finishing school in Switzerland, really, I suppose, to keep her away from Dennis. She's determined he won't succeed, and I must say that I'm on her side. One or two of her friends work as secretaries, and Cressida's wondering about enrolling in Secretarial College and getting a job. It'd certainly give her some independence, and I believe that's what she needs."

Sally nodded, in full agreement with Dalton Horwood's womenfolk in that respect, and they moved on to talk about other things. Before long, they heard footsteps in the hallway, and moments later Phil Winter put his head round the door.

"That about sums it up for now, Dakers. We'll be on our way. Mrs Horwood, your husband and I have had a full and frank discussion, and we believe a ransom demand will come to light, probably no later than today. Mr Horwood feels it's worth keeping an eye on Dennis Nolan, a suggestion which I'll act upon. Your husband will contact me as soon as he hears from your daughter's kidnappers."

Sally thanked Marjorie for the coffee and biscuits and followed Winter out to the car. She told him of the discussion they'd just had, and Marjorie's take on the situation. The DI was dismissive.

"Wouldn't set much store by that, Dakers. In my opinion, Dalton Horwood is a very discerning man. We'll head back to the station now, as there are some outstanding issues Don Pilling wants me to resolve. I don't think we need revisit the other interviewees, as DS Gallian and yourself seem to have done a thorough job there. Don assures me I can fully rely on you both."

"Thank you, sir." This was praise indeed, and on the back of it, Sally decided she'd give DI Winter a chance.

Back at the station, she had a quick lunch in the canteen before tackling the paperwork which had accumulated on her desk. DS Gallian and

DC Brady were likely to be out all day, Yvonne Begley told her, investigating the matter of the body found in the canal. She learned that the body was Jerry Rudd's, and even though she only knew him by reputation, Sally believed there'd be a long list of suspects for his murder.

It was much later in the day when she came out into the corridor to visit the Records office that she noticed a familiar face.

Dalton Horwood, looking frazzled and red-faced, was hopping impatiently from one foot to the other, trying to claim Tom Wrightson's attention, even though Tom was busy dealing with two people at the desk.

Sally approached the MP. "Mr Horwood?"

"Ah, yes. Is DI Winter around?"

"I'll take you to his office, sir. This way, please." She led the way down the corridor and, as she knocked on Winter's door, noticed that Horwood was holding a crumpled sheet of paper and seemed very much on edge.

"Come!"

Sally pushed open the door. "Sir, Mr Horwood..."

The MP had already burst past her, and Winter scrambled to his feet.

"They've made contact." He marched up to the desk and shoved the sheet of paper under the DI's nose. "Poked through the letter box in the fading light. Marjorie and I were alone in the house and didn't see or hear anything of the person who left it."

Deciding she was part of this investigation and feeling she should be treated as such, Sally made her way over to stand behind Winter's shoulder.

The letters of the ransom note had been cut from newspaper headlines. 'BRIDLE PATH TO BELDON WOODS, GARSTON LANE,' it read. '£5000 IN USED NOTES. 8PM TOMORROW. NO POLICE OR SHE SUFFERS.'

"Five thousand pounds!" Horwood was outraged. "I – I'll pay it, of course. But they – they want me to go alone?"

Sally could tell Horwood was scared, because the ransom note, with its glaring capitals, was loaded with menace. Her first thought was that the kidnappers weren't playing games; her second that, despite his pomposity and snobbishness, she felt sorry for Horwood, who, she believed, was genuinely fearful for his daughter's safety. And what of Marjorie? How might she be feeling at this moment? Sally's heart went out to her.

Winter took control, his manner reassuring. "Get the money together, sir," he advised. "We won't interfere, but I promise we *will* be on hand. You won't be alone. I need time to think this out, then I'll come over tomorrow morning to discuss it with you. Our first priority is to get Cressida back safely before we go after them. I'll keep this note and study the location, so that we can be nearby and unobserved. I must emphasize, however, that you tell no-one about this."

Horwood seemed to have recovered slightly and nodded his agreement. "Of course, Winter. Thank you. I'll see you in the morning."

He turned and strode out majestically, Sally holding the door for him, and Phil Winter resumed his seat, looking very pleased with himself. He dismissed her, telling her to be ready and waiting the following morning, by which time he'd have come up with a plan to keep tabs on the kidnappers once they'd released Cressida Horwood.

Back at her digs that evening, Sally phoned Jill Gallian. They had a pleasant chat, during which Jill invited Sally to her choir's performance of Handel's Messiah the following month, as well as the girls agreeing a date to meet in town for lunch. Neal was home, and Jill wondered if Sally wanted a word? Much as she liked Jill, that had been her real reason for phoning.

She gave Neal a quick summary of the kidnapping case. He'd begun the investigation with her, and it seemed only fair that he should be kept informed. After all, she doubted DI Winter would do it.

Neal agreed that Winter had made the right call. "How did you get on with him?" he asked.

"Oh, he's not so bad. Bit of a glory seeker, but I'd say he's efficient. And you? Yvonne said the body in the canal was Jerry Rudd's?"

"Yes, Mal and Pam are busy building a list of possible suspects."

"From what I've heard about Rudd, it'll be a long list."

"And that's just the beginning. Then we've got to seek them out and interview them. This looks like one of those investigations which is going to take some time."

12

The next morning, Neal called on Mick Jenner, licensee of The Boat, to ask if he'd accompany him to the mortuary to officially identify the body of Jerry Rudd. There were no relatives, at least none who could be traced, and he didn't want to inflict the task on Mrs Lynch, who was very elderly and the only person to seem at all saddened by Rudd's passing.

Mick Jenner confirmed that the body was Jerry's. "Yep, that's him alright. D'you know, Sergeant, I shall miss him in a funny sort of way. Likeable enough bloke, but he always struck me as being a bit shady."

It was an understated epitaph, and Neal withheld a smile. Jerry Rudd would have sold his grandmother's false teeth; might well have done so in one of his early incursions into villainy, assuming he'd had a grandmother.

Having dropped off Jenner, Neal drove back to the station and went along to update Phil Winter on progress. He'd already been in touch with DCI Pilling the previous evening, and it didn't sit well with him that in doing so, he was undermining Winter. However, Pilling was still his boss, far more experienced than any of them, and Neal knew he'd put him right if he felt he was heading down the wrong road.

"No great loss, if you ask me," Winter said, when Neal informed him that the canal victim was Jerry Rudd. "I remember him from my time in Oxford. Wouldn't trust him as far as I could throw him. I suspect one of his fellow conmen did him in – perhaps he'd queered someone's pitch. More likely it'd have been one of his victims. Still, it has to be investigated, even though other matters may take priority."

"You're probably right, Phil," Neal replied. "But I can't help thinking there may be more to it than that."

Winter grinned. "Don Pilling warned me about your gut feelings. He wanted me to include you on the Horwood case, but perhaps it's best for now if you concentrate on finding Rudd's killer. I've already drawn up a plan for getting Cressida Horwood back safely and thwarting the kidnappers. Perhaps we'll agree to keep one another informed on a daily basis?"

In other words, Winter didn't want him anywhere near the Horwood case. He noticed an Ordnance Survey map for the Oxford area spread across the DI's desk with various red markings on it in bold red pen. Well, it suited Neal. He and his team had more than enough to keep them occupied.

On leaving the DI's office, he encountered a familiar figure giving Tom Wrightson grief at the front desk. "I'm sorry, Mr Rackham," Tom was saying, making every effort to remain patient. "DI Winter's extremely busy at the moment. If there's a statement to be made, I'm sure he'll let you know in due course."

With his door still open, Winter had had no problem hearing his name mentioned and came striding out. "Something the matter, Tom?"

Tom looked up in exasperation as he guessed the rug was about to be pulled from under his feet. "Mr Rackham was asking to see you, sir. I explained -."

Larry Rackham saw an opening and was quick to exploit it. "Word's got around that someone's topped Jerry Rudd, Inspector. I was wondering if you might be able to give me a few details?"

"Do you want me to do that, Phil?" Neal asked, sharing a glance with Tom, in the hope he might be able to send Rackham on his way with the bare minimum.

A forlorn hope, as it turned out.

"Thanks, Neal," came Winter's reply. "But I'm sure I can spare Mr Rackham a few minutes."

Larry was suddenly enlivened. "I'd really appreciate a word with you, Mr Winter. I mean, here you are back in Oxford and the man in charge." He cast a swift, dismissive glance at Tom Wrightson. "Must tell me all about your time in the Met. Pretty exciting stuff, I should reckon?"

Winter glowed with self-satisfaction, lapping up the flattery. It was an unfortunate moment for Sally Dakers to emerge from Neal's office. "Just a few minutes, then, Mr Rackham. As Sergeant Wrightson pointed out, I'm extremely busy. Ah, Dakers, perhaps you'd fetch us each a coffee from the canteen?"

"White with three sugars, love," Rackham piped up.

Looking resigned, Sally replied "Yes, sir," and went off to do the honours, while Winter strode magnificently back to his office, with Rackham shuffling along respectfully in his wake.

Tom looked on, unimpressed. "Best not to give someone like Rackham an inch," he growled. "And the Wonder Boy'll give him more than that, I'll be bound. Mark my words, Neal, he'll learn the hard way."

Just then, Mal Brady sloped in. "Morning, Gally. Have a word?" He sounded much more businesslike than usual, and Neal was alert to Tom's raised eyebrows.

"Sure, Mal. Let's go into the office."

He led the way and pointed his colleague to a seat. "How's it going?"

"Think I might have something. Remember Kelvin Gorse?"

Gorse was a serial offender, in and out of jail like a yo-yo. "Isn't he inside?" Neal asked.

"He's out, as of last week. But a couple of years back, when you were out of action, Jerry Rudd tipped us off about some job Gorse was pulling, and Taff and Hodge went along there and caught him in the act. You know Jerry – always tried to keep under the radar. But what if Gorse had got a sniff that it was Jerry who'd shopped him? He'd be out for revenge."

"Sounds promising, Mal," Neal replied, "and worth checking out. So, let's find Gorse."

"Might be easier said than done, Gally. They're a big family, spread over Oxford. He could be with any of 'em."

"Sit here and make a list. I'll find out how Pam's doing at her end, then come and help you track down Gorse. This may be the opening we're looking for."

*

Jill Gallian was window shopping in the city centre and feeling rather fed up. She'd noticed several items she'd have liked to buy: some pillowcases in Elliston & Cavell's, a table lamp in Boswell's, a pair of court shoes in Manfield. But she hadn't enough money on her for any of these without cashing a cheque, and the problem was that Neal had their cheque book, having offered to visit a bank that lunchtime. Why, oh why hadn't she said she'd cash the cheque? But it had slipped her mind, and she'd only remembered once he'd left for work. What had happened to the super-efficient Jill Westmacott of Briar Hedge, so used to doing all the thinking for her uncle? Married life, she supposed, and daydreaming of her husband when he wasn't beside her, viewing the world through rose-tinted spectacles. Oh well, she supposed, life wasn't so bad, and she could purchase those items another day.

 Jill first noticed the woman as she was looking through the display of table lamps in Boswell's: a small woman in a dowdy brown raincoat and flat shoes, a silk scarf covering her head and what looked like an empty shopping bag in her hand. She looked up and smiled as Jill walked past her, and Jill returned the smile a little uncertainly.

 She noticed her again in Sainsbury's at Carfax, when she was at the counter buying ham for Neal's sandwiches and some stewing beef for the next two nights' casserole. The woman wasn't buying anything, just standing near the door and looking. Looking, Jill thought, at her. And she was sure that when she'd cut through the Covered Market to buy a copy of *Woman's Weekly*, the same woman had been a few yards behind her. Or had she? Or was Jill simply imagining things?

 Feeling somewhat uncomfortable, Jill decided it was time to head home. Quickening her pace, she crossed the road and hurried down Queen Street to queue for a bus. As luck would have it, one bound for Headington had just drawn up, and Jill tagged on to the end of the queue. The line of passengers started to shunt forward, and she went with them, just at that moment feeling a hand upon her arm.

 She looked down at the woman in the brown raincoat, who was smiling up at her hopefully. "Excuse me, dear," she said. "Can you spare a minute?"

 "I'm sorry," Jill replied, as she edged closer to the bus's open doors. "But I really do have to get home."

 She felt spooked. The woman had been following her, possibly from the moment she'd arrived in Cornmarket Street.

"Oh, I see." The hand dropped away, and Jill felt the smile was tinged with sadness, as the woman backed away from the queue to stand in the middle of the pavement. And she immediately felt a pang of guilt for having snubbed her.

The bus was fairly crowded and, as Jill got on and moved along the lower deck, she looked back and saw her follower standing where she'd left her, staring after her intently with a wistful look. A man arose, doffed his hat and offered Jill his seat. She smiled, thanked him and sat down. As the bus lurched away, the woman raised a hand in a forlorn wave, her smile sadder than before. Jill thought she had to have mistaken her for someone else.

*

Neal returned home that evening after a busy day trawling across the city speaking to acquaintances – there were no friends – of the late Jerry Rudd. Pam Harding and her young colleague had worked hard but had drawn a blank. When Neal caught up with them, he stood them both a cup of tea and cream bun and told them to give it another hour before calling it a day.

He and Mal Brady had called in on several members of the Gorse family, but no-one knew where Kelvin was, or if they did, they weren't telling – which he strongly suspected to be the case where Gorse's mother and brother were concerned. The father would have been no help: he was currently inside, charged with breaking and entering, a dubious talent which seemed to run in the family.

He was glad to get home, particularly with Jill greeting him at the door of their flat and leading him into the kitchen, where the delicious aroma of the casserole made his mouth water. She poured him a glass of beer, said supper wouldn't be long, took him into the sitting room, sat down beside him and asked about his day.

He told her, sparing her the least interesting details, and asked what she'd been doing.

"Oh, there was a woman in Oxford following me around – I'm sure she must have mistaken me for someone else. But it's nothing to worry about, because there's something else I need to ask you. You see, there were several things I'd have liked to buy, but I didn't have enough money. You did remember to cash that cheque, though, didn't you?"

"Ah…"

Jill sighed. "Oh, Neal! Well, it's my fault anyway. I should have taken the cheque book because I knew I was going into town. Please, can you do it tomorrow? I realize you're busy but *please* don't forget. I need to pay the plumber, and he won't accept a cheque."

"I promise I won't forget," he assured her. "I'll pop into the branch in Walton Street because I shall be working down that way."

Jill tried to look stern. "Well, make sure you do."

"Or you might pitch me out on my ear?"

She smiled as she snuggled up to him. "D'you know, I doubt if it'll come to that? Somehow, I think I'd rather hang on to you."

13

Sally was summoned to Phil Winter's office the moment Larry Rackham had left.

"Ah, Dakers. We'll be on our way. I want to carry out a quick recce of tonight's location before we go on to Farway House."

This time, Winter drove. She guessed he wanted to be seen as the man in complete charge of an important operation. They used an unmarked car, not wanting to advertise a police presence, even though the appointed time was several hours away. Heaven forbid that people seeing them travelling together would think that she was his girlfriend – or even his wife!

Sally hadn't been involved in the planning, which Winter had kept to himself. The location was a narrow country lane, bordered by a copse on one side and fields leading to dense woodland on the other, with no farms or cottages in sight.

Winter was looking pleased with himself. "All just as I'd hoped," he commented. Sally was looking understandably puzzled. "You'll get a full briefing once we're at Farway House, Dakers," he added.

Once there, they were met at the door by both Horwoods. Sally wondered immediately if they'd given Mrs Davis the day off, to ensure she knew as little as possible about what was happening. The MP, smartly suited, looked businesslike, Marjorie pale and apprehensive. She and Sally exchanged a brief smile, Horwood and Winter already marching purposefully towards the study.

The DI unfurled his map across Horwood's wide, uncluttered desk, and the two men bent their heads over it, while the women stood back and looked on. Winter jabbed a finger importantly at several places he'd marked in red on the map.

"Drive alone to the gateway to this field, sir," he said. "Get out of the car and wait for them to show up. As you can see, they've chosen an isolated spot and can only access it from either end of the lane. I shall have a squad car concealed at either end, and they'll both be in radio contact with me."

"I know they said to come alone," Horwood put in. "But will there be no-one on hand?" He seemed for once uncertain, and Sally saw no trace of his previous bluster.

"WDC Dakers and I will be in the bushes directly opposite the gateway," Winter assured him confidently, leaving Sally hoping that Yvonne and Pam never got to learn that she'd been in the bushes with the DI. She wasn't sure how Paul Hodgson might take it either.

"You're surely not going to tackle them while I'm there?" Horwood's alarm was apparent.

"We'll merely observe them, Mr Horwood, and note the car's registration number. Once your daughter's been released, and they have the money, we let them drive off to be intercepted by the squad car at the end of the lane, while the other drives up behind them."

"Please, Dalton, do as DI Winter says," Marjorie pleaded. "Don't try to be a hero."

Sally felt there'd be little chance of that. At that moment, the MP was looking decidedly paler than his wife.

But he spoke with some of his customary authority. "I want our daughter back too, Marjorie. Her safety is paramount. I'm satisfied with the inspector's plan. And I take it, Winter," he went on, "that you'll be keeping a close eye on our Mr Nolan?"

"I shall have an officer on the beat passing along Blackhall Road every ten minutes," the DI declared, and Sally silently congratulated him for thinking on his feet – it was the first she'd heard of it. She noticed that Marjorie was looking exasperated and found herself hoping there was no way Dennis Nolan could be mixed up in this.

It was early afternoon by the time they got back to the station, and Winter called two of the squad car crews and Sally together for a briefing, carefully pointing out where he wanted them to take up their positions and what he expected them to do.

"The two directions you'll be covering are the only way they can get to the rendezvous point," he said. "There are paths through the woods, but none of them are wide enough for a car."

He dismissed everyone, ordering them to be in position by six p.m., before sending Sally off on a well-earned break. She decided to go out for a late lunch, because a long evening seemed in prospect.

It kicked off early, just as darkness was setting in, and it was Sally who took the call and hurried along to his office to give DI Winter the message.

"PC Palgrave's just called in, sir. He was turning into Blackhall Road when he saw a woman going into Dennis Nolan's building. A young man answering Nolan's description opened the door to her."

Winter was quickly out of his chair. "I knew it – his accomplice! Looks like Mr Horwood was right. Come on, Dakers. There's a chance we can nip this in the bud and save him his five thousand pounds."

It was Sally's duty to follow her superior's instructions. But she had misgivings. Palgrave hadn't had a proper glimpse of the woman, who could be Dennis Nolan's mother for all they knew. But – hers not to reason why. As they dashed out to the yard, Sally five yards in arrears of the energized Winter, she registered Tom Wrightson's surprise and controlled smirk of amusement.

Winter was already behind the wheel and starting up. He deployed the siren to carve a path through Cornmarket and Broad Street, both which had their share of homebound traffic, but switched it off once they were in Parks Road. They drew up some fifty yards distant from Nolan's building.

Jon Palgrave crossed the road to meet them, young, nervous and in awe of the DI from London.

"I'd just turned the corner from Parks Road, sir, when I saw a young man open the door and a woman go in. I only had a back view of her. It was too dark to see much else."

Winter was expansive. "You did well to call it in, Constable. Right, you can continue your beat. I'll take it from here." He crossed the road in long strides, forcing Sally to scurry after him but with time to recognize the vehicle parked a little way down the neighbouring road.

Winter rapped authoritatively on the front door, and after a brief delay Dennis Nolan pulled it open. He looked surprised, never having met the DI, but relaxed visibly on noticing Sally.

"DI Winter, Mr Nolan." His voice radiated triumph. "I -er, do believe you have a visitor?"

"Um, yes," Dennis replied. "Would you like to come in?" Unseen by Winter, he and Sally exchanged a quick smile.

Winter stood aside to allow the boy to lead them down a short flight of stairs and through the open door of the basement flat. As the visitor rose from her seat to greet him, he pulled up as if he'd been shot.

"Oh – Mrs Horwood."

"Good afternoon, Inspector. Oh, and WDC Dakers." She indicated a round tin on the coffee table before her. "I hope you don't mind me calling in on Dennis to bring him some fruit cake. I busied myself with some baking earlier to occupy my mind."

"Oh, ah, yes," Winter harrumphed, a habit he seemed to have caught from a certain MP. "Er, well, as long as all's in order, Mrs Horwood. Dakers and I will be getting along and, hopefully, we can secure your daughter's release in the next few hours."

"I trust so," Marjorie replied. "Thank you, Inspector. We'll be praying that all goes well."

"We're sure it will, Mrs Horwood," Sally said with a reassuring smile, as her superior seemed lost for words, an inane grin pasted on his face in a woeful effort to cover his embarrassment.

*

Winter ensured that everyone was in position by six o'clock. One of the cars had dropped him and Sally at the top of the lane, and they walked back along it to a spot directly opposite the gateway where the meeting was to take place. To Sally's dismay, the DI had again referred to the two of them being concealed in the bushes, and as she'd got out of the car, she'd steadfastly ignored Paul Hodgson's wink and his colleague's thumbs-up.

They endured a long, cold wait, the minutes dripping by. The night was very still, and the lane seemed miles distant from civilization. Eventually, a Land Rover came into view and pulled up on the verge. Sally recognized the registration number as belonging to the vehicle Marjorie had driven on her visit to Dennis Nolan that afternoon. She pictured her waiting at home, the anxious mother unable to settle to anything, straining for the sound of the Land Rover to herald her daughter's safe return, peering down the dark driveway for a redeeming glimpse of it.

Dalton Horwood climbed out, reaching back to pick up a small suitcase. He closed the door, looked around and checked his watch. Sally glanced at hers. Ten minutes to eight. Horwood wore a thick overcoat and gloves, but she saw him shiver and shift uneasily from foot to foot, stamping on the hard ground in an effort to keep out the cold.

Winter's walkie-talkie crackled, and he snatched it from his pocket. Paul Hodgson's voice sounded tinny and very distant.

"A car just passed us, sir. Should be with you any minute."

"Roger, Car One. Cars One and Two hold your positions. I'll tell you when to close in. No more contact now."

The DI and Sally listened out for the car's approach. They heard it from some way off, but its engine seemed to be idling. Then the sound cut out.

"He's stopped along the lane," Winter whispered. "Coming the rest of the way on foot, it would seem."

But Sally's attention was elsewhere, and she snatched at his sleeve. "Look, sir." She pointed to the open gateway, beyond which a dark figure loomed, face obscured by a cartoon mask. He'd appeared so suddenly, as if out of nowhere, and she saw Dalton Horwood start as he became aware of the man's presence. Farther back in the field, a similarly clad man was holding back a slightly built, struggling, blonde-haired girl.

"Got the money, mush?" The kidnapper's voice seemed to boom out of the stillness.

Horwood looked wildly around as if expecting assistance, although Winter had briefed him thoroughly that morning. "It – it's all here." He held up the suitcase, his voice thin, emasculated.

"Give it here, then."

"I want my daughter first."

"Just give it here, pal, will you?" The figure lunged forward, grabbing at the suitcase, and Horwood, suddenly emboldened, snatched it back out of reach, the man stumbling against him. "My daughter first!" he shouted.

Winter, anticipating problems, began to move, but Sally clamped a hand on his wrist, holding him back. At that same moment, they were made aware of a frenzied rustling in the bushes some way along from them, followed by a stifled cry and flash of light.

"Here!" the second man yelled from the field. "He's brought the bleedin' cops!"

His companion, still trying in vain to wrest the case from Horwood's jealous grasp, shoved the MP away so that he fell backwards on to the verge. Then he turned and ran back into the field, both kidnappers hustling the girl along between them.

Sally heard footsteps in the lane, someone running away. She started to alert Winter, but he was already gone, hurtling across the road and into the field, giving chase. Sally followed, stopping to help a red-faced Horwood to his feet.

"You ruined it!" he yelled. "Your stupid idiot in the bushes ruined it! I'll have the whole damned lot of you sacked!"

He'd recovered his voice, and then some. Even so, his ravings were drowned out by the roar of a motorbike. For a moment, Sally was afraid it might be heading their way, but its sound quickly faded, and seconds later the figure of the returning DI loomed out of the darkness, busy on his walkie-talkie.

"They've made off through the woods…no, too narrow…motorbike and sidecar…Car Two, get out on to the main road…alert anyone else in the vicinity…three people…yes, Car One, bring him here. Over and out."

Dalton Horwood was practically treading on his toes by the time he'd finished giving his instructions. "How do you explain this, Winter?" he bawled. "It had better be good, or I'll make sure you're pounding the beat by the end of the week!"

Phil Winter wasn't Sally's favourite person, and she knew she spoke for most if not all her colleagues. In the two days he'd been at

Oxford, he couldn't be said to have made a good impression, but she was full of admiration for him then. He answered the MP with both dignity and respect, even though, like her, he was probably quaking inside.

"I'm sorry, Mr Horwood. But I can assure you the interruption was not down to any member of my team. There seems to have been someone concealed in the bushes further along the lane. He tried to make off, but my men have intercepted him."

Before Horwood could form a reply, a squad car appeared and drew up alongside them. Paul Hodgson climbed out of the back seat dragging a forlorn, dishevelled figure after him. The man's face bore numerous scratches, inflicted by his sojourn in the bushes, and a camera dangled from around his neck.

"Rackham!" Winter's face was like thunder.

"Then -," Horwood exclaimed, "this is not one of your men? If not, who the devil is he?"

"I'm sorry." Larry Rackham's voice was shorn of its customary bravado. "I – I tripped on a root. I only came along to observe…"

"With your knowledge, Winter?" Horwood stormed.

"*Without* my knowledge, sir. He's a journalist and had no right to be here. I've no idea how he got to know about this operation."

There'd been a slight pause in the middle of the DI's last sentence. Only Sally seemed to have picked up on and guessed the reason for it. Winter had openly invited Larry Rackham into his office that morning, and the eagle-eyed journalist wouldn't have missed the map with its red markings spread across his desk. Again, she admired Winter for thinking on his feet.

"I don't know how you got hold of this, Rackham. But I warn you that if you print so much as a word about tonight or mention this matter to anyone, I shall arrest and charge you with compromising a police operation. Is there a film in that camera? Take it out and give it to me."

With quivering hands, Rackham did as he was asked, and Winter exposed the film before dropping it into his overcoat pocket.

Dalton Horwood was simmering at his shoulder. "Who do you work for, man?" he barked. "I'll have you sacked. And who put you up to this?"

"I'm freelance," Rackham squeaked. "And I can't divulge my source." Sally noted the shifty glance he darted at Phil Winter.

"Get out of my sight," Winter ordered. "I'll see you in my office tomorrow at nine sharp, and after that you won't be welcome in my station ever again. Is that clear?"

"Clear, Mr Winter."

The DI nodded to Hodgson, who took Rackham by the arm and escorted him back along the road to where he'd left his car.

He was alert to the fact that Horwood hadn't finished with him and drew him aside, beyond where Sally stood.

"I'd be grateful if you'd let me deal with that matter, sir," he said. "As to the kidnappers, I was on the point of intervening when the interruption occurred. In my opinion, they were about to take the money without handing over your daughter."

"Humph! I fail to see how you can reach that conclusion, Winter. You're snatching at straws, if you ask me."

Sally, well within earshot, felt, however, that the same idea had occurred to the MP, who no longer seemed to be baying for blood.

"They didn't get the money, Mr Horwood," the DI went on. "By that token, they'll try again, and very soon."

"Then I hope for your sake that you're right, Winter. Otherwise, you'll be explaining yourself to Clive Streatley." He turned and marched back to the Land Rover, got in, slammed the door and sped off, his face grim.

Car Two called in to report no sighting of the motorbike and sidecar, but it had been a forlorn hope anyway.

Winter and Sally returned to Oxford in the squad car, the DI requesting that she be dropped off at her digs and having the grace to thank her for all her efforts that day. Apart from that, he hardly said a word on the way back, and she felt the evening's events had proved a heavy blow to his pride.

14

Having finished tidying the flat the following morning, Jill made herself a sandwich for lunch and then walked down to the grocer's shop at the bottom of the hill to buy some flour. She'd decided to make a jam sponge to follow the rest of the casserole she'd heat up for her and Neal's tea. There was very little money in her purse, and she hoped he'd have remembered to go to the bank and cash a cheque, although she understood how busy he was, chasing across Oxford with his scruffy little DC, interviewing suspects. She'd gathered there were quite a few, because the man they'd fished out of the canal hadn't seemed to be anyone's favourite person.

Jill made her purchase, and on her way back up the hill realized that someone was waiting outside the gate to their building. On drawing nearer, she recognized the brown raincoat as belonging to the woman who'd been following her around in the city centre the previous day. The gate gave on to the front entrance to the flats, so the woman was effectively barring her way. As no-one happened to be passing by, Jill knew there was nothing else for it but to confront her.

As she approached, the woman turned towards her with a smile. "Hello, my dear. I thought that must be you coming up the hill. I'd just got off the bus at the top of the road, when I chanced to see you coming out of your gate. It must be my lucky day."

Jill had decided to cut to the chase. "I'm sorry," she said tartly, "but I don't know who you are. And may I ask why you were following me around yesterday, as well as coming looking for me today?"

The woman's smile moved up a notch. "But I believe I'm your mother, dear."

Jill shook her head adamantly. Her mother, as far as she knew, was back at her school in Kenya, she'd seen her a little over a month ago, and she didn't bear any resemblance to the dowdy little woman standing in front of her.

"I'm afraid you're mistaken," Jill said.

"I'm Anne Barcham, dear." The woman seemed undeterred, as if by her patience she might persuade Jill to change her mind.

"As I've said, Mrs Barcham, I'm sorry, but I don't know you."

"I was sure, of course, that you wouldn't remember me. You're my little Jeanie, and you weren't quite five years old when he took you away from me. My, you've grown into such a pretty girl."

"Mrs Barcham, please listen to me. You're *not* my mother. My name's Jill Gallian, my maiden name was Westmacott, and my parents are Ben and Janet, who are currently teaching at a school in Kenya."

Anne Barcham's answer was to dig into the worn-looking handbag hanging from her shoulder and bring out a crumpled black-and-white photograph which she presented to Jill. "And that's not you, you say? But I was so sure it must be, the moment I saw you." Her voice had lost some of its previous assurance and most of its misplaced hope.

Out of politeness, Jill took hold of the photograph and glanced at it. The gap-toothed little girl with her fair hair in bunches bore a passing resemblance to her, but that was all. She'd had Anne Barcham down as a crank but now, as the woman waited, patient and pathetic, on her reply, she felt she was merely confused and reasoned that she was harmless.

"Where do you live, Mrs Barcham?" she asked.

"Silver Birches in Cowley."

Jill knew of it: a care home for mentally disturbed people. She handed back the photograph. "That's not me," she said softly.

Anne Barcham looked downcast, and her dejection went to Jill's heart. "Come inside," she suggested on impulse, "and I'll make you a cup of tea."

"Oh, my dear, that'd be so kind."

Jill opened the gate and ushered the woman up the path, just as the door opened and Mrs Stone from the downstairs flat looked out. Neal and Jill liked their elderly neighbours, who'd quickly taken to them, and she knew that not much got past Mrs Stone, who must have been watching from her sitting room window.

She was looking concerned. "Is everything alright, Mrs Gallian?" she asked.

"Fine, Mrs Stone," Jill replied, smiling. "This lady's Mrs Barcham, and she's got me confused with someone else. I'm just taking her upstairs for a cup of tea."

"If you're sure, dear? Do call down if you need me."

Jill nodded her thanks and led her new friend up the stairs and into the flat. She took the precaution of leaving her front door open, grateful that Mrs Stone would be on guard duty downstairs.

She sat Anne Barcham on the sofa, made tea, put a few biscuits on a plate and took them through to where the woman was eyeing her surroundings with something like awe.

"This is a lovely little flat, my dear." She indicated the framed wedding photograph in the centre of the mantelpiece. "Is that you with your husband? It looks quite recent."

"Yes, it was taken just two months ago."

"He must be so proud to have married a lovely girl like you."

Jill found herself blushing at the compliment and busied herself searching in the cupboard for her photograph album, in the hope of setting the matter straight once and for all.

She went and sat beside the woman, opened the album and showed photographs of herself as a toddler posing with her parents towards the end of the war, her dad in army uniform.

Anne Barcham looked at her with an air of apology. "Oh dear. Obviously, I've made a mistake. I'm so sorry to have put you out. I hope you're not angry with me?"

Jill smiled reassuringly. "Of course I'm not angry. But I don't think it's the first time you've been mistaken, is it?"

Anne shook her head ruefully. "No, dear, it's not. And people haven't always been as understanding as you. I'm always looking out for Jeanie, you see. My husband took her away – she wasn't quite five years old, and I've never seen either of them again."

"But where did he take her?"

"Away – I don't know where."

"And you've never heard from him at all?"

"Never, although I did hear that he died some time ago. But I feel sure my Jeanie's still alive. I shall go on looking for her, and I hope that one day I'll find her."

They finished their tea, and Anne got up to leave. "I'd better get the bus back to Cowley now. Thank you, dear. You've been so kind."

Jill offered to accompany her back to the bus stop and, feeling desperately sorry for her, asked Anne if she'd like her to come and call on her at Silver Birches one day soon?

"Oh, thank you. Yes. That'd be lovely."

Mrs Stone was waiting in her doorway, having heard them on the stairs. She looked anxious, and Jill explained that she was walking Mrs Barcham to the bus stop at the top of the road.

She waited with Anne for a bus to come along, saw her on to it and waved her off, hoping at least that, if only temporarily, she'd set the poor woman's mind at rest.

Mrs Stone was waiting by the gate when Jill returned.

"I've seen her around, poor soul," she said. "That must be the woman whose husband took their daughter off with some vague promise of going on holiday – oh, years ago, it was. The police looked for them but never found the girl. He died, and I seem to recall there was something suspicious about his death. The poor woman suffered a breakdown. Lived with her mother, but when she died, she had to go into a home. That was very sweet and trusting of you to take her in, Mrs Gallian."

"She was following me around in town the other day," Jill explained. "She saw me get on the Headington bus and must have come here on the off chance of finding me. She thought I might be her daughter."

Mrs Stone's reply was interrupted by the noise of a vehicle screeching to a halt at the kerb. They opened the door, and Jill, looking out, immediately recognized her uncle's battered old Land Rover. Colonel Wilkie scrambled out and scurried to the gate.

"Uncle Lam!" Jill called out. "Whatever's the matter?"

Wilkie was looking unusually frazzled. "I've tried phoning you, Jill," he replied, "but I guess you must have been out. I take it you've not heard the news?"

"What news?"

"There's been a bank hold-up in town. There've been gunshots, and the police are involved…"

"Where, exactly?" As Jill gasped out the words, a dark sense of foreboding crept up on her.

"A branch in Walton Street."

She immediately went cold all over, startling Mrs Stone, who flung an arm around her.

"But – but Neal -?" The words sounded distant, intoned by a disembodied voice which surely wasn't hers. "N-Neal's there. He's been making inquiries down in that area. He was – was going to call into the branch in Walton Street because I – I'd asked him to…"

Jill was aware of Mrs Stone conferring with her uncle as he approached down the path, his face gaunt with concern.

"Perhaps we should go inside and phone the station, Mrs Gallian," her neighbour suggested. "Come along, dear. You can use my phone."

And Jill, feeling that her growing distress might easily overwhelm her, knew she had to stay strong and decided that she couldn't remain where she was, waiting in trepidation, fighting to hold back tears.

"No, Mrs Stone. I won't phone. I-I'll go down there. I – I must know. Uncle Lam, please, will you -?"

Colonel Wilkie took her by the arm. "Of course, my dear. I'll drive you down to the station right away."

15

For Neal and his team, luck slowly began to turn their way in the search for Jerry Rudd's killer. The previous evening, a police constable on his beat in Botley passed a white Cortina coming out of a side road on one of the estates. As it drove away, he happened to notice the row of Butlin's stickers in the back window. Remembering one of the many instructions the beat officers had been given, he made a note of the registration number, hurried to the nearest police call box and reported it in. Unfortunately, the car had been there and gone so quickly, he'd had no chance to notice anything about the driver.

The duty sergeant passed Neal the information on his arrival at the station that morning, and the moment Yvonne Begley appeared, Neal asked her to track down the details of the car's owner and report back to him. The call from the Botley constable had been logged at just after 11pm. So, had the driver been visiting someone who lived on the estate, or might he be a resident? If the car had been registered locally, it wouldn't take long for Yvonne to find out.

*

A second stroke of good fortune wasn't long in arriving. Pam Harding was down in the Jericho area that morning continuing inquiries concerning acquaintances of the late Jerry Rudd who might have held a grudge against him. As Pam rounded a street corner, a young lad ran into her at full pelt.

Pam was a sturdy lass, the boy short and skinny, and he bounced off her to land firmly on his backside. His mate came panting along after him. The one had been chasing the other, and when the second boy saw what had happened, he pulled up abruptly, an expression of guilt on his face.

When Pam saw what he was holding, she could understand why. As the first boy scrambled to his feet, she grabbed him by the arm and beckoned his mate towards her. He seemed reluctant, but Pam had a remedy for that. "Get here now when I tell you!" she ordered him sternly.

He shuffled forward, and she pointed at the object in his hand.

"Where did you get that? Come on, hand it over, and be quick about it!"

Pam fished an envelope from the pocket of her uniform, opened it out and got the boy to drop in the wooden-handled, thin-bladed letter opener he'd been clutching.

"Well?" she demanded.

Both boys were staring down at their scuffed and muddy shoes. "Found it along the canal, miss," said one. "Off the tow path, right underneath the bank. He shoved me," he directed a desultory nod at his mate, "and I nearly fell in."

"But we wasn't doing nothing with it, miss," the second lad piped up. "Just larking about on our way to school, like. Didn't mean no harm, and we would've handed it in, honest…"

A likely story.

"Well, consider it handed in now," Pam replied. "And you're going to be late for school, because I have to get a detective here to talk to you about this. So, you two just follow me along to the call box and behave yourselves while I get him down here."

*

Neal reacted swiftly to Pam's call, hauling a reluctant Brady from the canteen and driving them down to where she was waiting with the boys.

"D'you reckon it's the weapon we're after?" Pam asked, once Neal had questioned the boys, and Mal was standing over them in case they had the idea of bunking off. But it seemed they were too mindful of incurring the wrath of Pam to try to escape.

"Could well be," Neal replied. "It's the right type of blade, after all, and they found it half a mile or so from where Rudd's body turned up. We'll see what forensics make of it, although any relevant prints will have been washed off."

He thanked the boys and left them in Pam's tender care. She'd give them another no-nonsense lecture as she accompanied them to their school to explain to their headmaster why they were late.

After that and before delivering the assumed weapon to forensics, Neal had asked her to call in on a few stationery stores to see if they could identify the make and model and ask if any assistants could recall having sold one recently. The latter was a long shot, but as Neal had found in the past, long shots could work in their favour. He sensed Pam's silent sigh: *more* legwork.

Neal and Mal Brady were having little success in tracing the whereabouts of the recently released Kelvin Gorse. He'd gone to ground, which suggested he might well be in the frame for Rudd's murder. There was a sizeable criminal element among the Gorse family, and the police weren't used to receiving any favours from them. As Neal had explained to those he'd interviewed, he simply wanted to cross Kelvin off the list of suspects. But so far, that approach had got him nowhere.

Before leaving Jericho, he realized he'd better do something about cashing a cheque, so that Jill could settle the plumber's bill. It had completely slipped his mind the previous day, and he wondered if it would make better sense for her to have charge of the cheque book, as she'd have more need of it in looking after their home. But first things first: get to the bank and cash a cheque!

They'd left the car nearby, and when he told Brady he was just popping along to the bank before they moved on, his colleague agreed to walk up there with him. Mal was shaking his head cynically. "That's marriage for you, Gally. A life spent under the thumb. One of the reasons I've steered clear of it."

Neal grinned, knowing it would need a special sort of woman to take on Mal Brady, beginning with his personal appearance. But he had to admit that Mal, although still some way off smart, was looking slightly less dishevelled than normally, probably owing to his ticking off from Phil Winter the other day.

"Too late for me to change now, Mal," he replied cheerfully. "And besides, I wouldn't want to."

The bank, a small branch, was situated along a parade of shops in Walton Street. As they crossed the road towards it, Neal happened to notice a car idling at the kerb some fifty yards away. Possibly the passenger had nipped into one of the shops…

He gave it no more thought, telling Mal to wait outside, as he didn't expect to be in there for more than a few minutes. But from the moment he'd pushed through the doors, he realized that something was badly wrong.

An elderly man in a bank guard's uniform sat slumped in a chair at the side of the counter, with a middle-aged woman kneeling anxiously beside him. Two others, a man and a woman, stood beyond them, huddled together and looking very frightened.

Neal's gaze switched to the counter where a man stood, his face covered by a hood and only his eyes visible. Those eyes, swift and cruel, were now trained on Neal, as was the cumbersome revolver in his hand.

"Get in here," he snarled. "Up against the wall with them and keep your trap shut." A holdall lay on the counter, behind which stood a trembling cashier. "Fill it up," the robber ordered. "Make it snappy, and no tricks."

Neal did as he'd been told, calculating the risk of any action and dismissing the thought in the same moment. He prayed silently that Brady wouldn't get fed up with waiting and wander in. The robber was on edge, and Neal didn't want anything to happen which would spook him into firing wildly. He shuddered at the prospect of the damage the bullets in that heavy gun might do.

With quivering hands, the cashier began to load the holdall, transferring bundles of banknotes from the small safe behind him. An older man, possibly the branch manager, stood to the side of him, his hands raised above his head, his face pale and anxious. The robber's gaze darted between the two bank employees, before coming to rest on Neal, the eyes narrowing dangerously.

"You're a copper, ain't you?" he growled. "Yeah, I seen you around. Well, pal, you stay right where you are, or you'll be the first to get it. Understand?" He clocked the empty safe. "Zip the bag up," he ordered the cashier.

The young man did as he was bid, a wave of the gun persuading him to step back from the counter. The robber transferred it to his other hand and swept up the holdall. He backed along the counter, the gun trained all the while on Neal. Without another word, he barged through the swing doors.

As they began to close behind him, Neal moved. "Call the police and ambulance," he ordered, as he hurried to the doors.

He would tell himself later that he should have taken his time, should simply have gone to the doors, noted the registration number of the car which had been waiting down the street and called it in. It was highly likely that it had been stolen, but even so, a patrol car might spot it and discover where it was heading.

Yet almost without thinking, he was following his instinct. As he emerged into the street, where people were scattering in all directions and taking refuge in the shops, the car was moving towards the bank, the robber waiting nervously for it, holdall in one hand, revolver in the other. Distracted by the movement, his head snapped round to face Neal, and he raised the gun.

Neal could never have guessed how many thoughts might rattle across his mind in the space of milliseconds, accompanied by a swirling kaleidoscope of faces: Jill, his late parents, his brother Roger, Clyde Holt, Helen, Tom Wrightson, Don Pilling.

He stood frozen to the spot, in no way able to move, preparing to be shot for the third and last time in the line of duty. He felt certain that one day Jill must marry again, hopefully to someone who'd put her at the very centre of his life and never flirt with danger, never give fate the opportunity to overwhelm and casually erase him. How, too, could he even momentarily have forgotten what had happened to Clyde?

He was staring down the barrel of the gun, his executioner not five yards away, his small eyes deadly, finger closing over the trigger with agonizing slowness and certainty…

Suddenly, the man was blasted sideways, the gun vaulting from his grasp to land on the pavement close to Neal's feet, as something resembling a scruffy, mackintoshed cannonball slammed into him, bulldozing him to the ground. Neal heard the sound of the man's head striking the pavement, as the not insubstantial weight of Mal Brady landed on top of him. The robber was going nowhere.

But the car was, first pulling in then screeching away from the kerb, giving Neal a glimpse of the alarm on the driver's face. Stunned into action, he crouched, picked up the gun and took aim. The shot blew out one of the rear tyres, and the car swerved across the road to smash head-on into a lamp post, steam spewing from beneath the crumpled bonnet. Neal ran across, tugged open the front door and hauled the groggy driver from his seat, shoved him face down to the ground and cuffed his hands behind his back.

The sound of the shot had temporarily deafened him, although he was sure he could hear the muffled sound of applause and cheering. He lifted the driver to his feet and propped him against the stricken car, suddenly grinning as he had a proper look at him for the first time.

"Kelvin," he gasped. "Fancy bumping into you."

16

Neal felt he was simply going through the motions as he tried to bring some order to the crime scene. There was a surreal quality to the situation, he and Mal the reluctant actors, and the small band of onlookers who'd emerged from the shelter of the shops were the extras, looking on pale and stunned.

Mal recognized the now unhooded gunman as Eddie Hannigan, Kelvin Gorse's cousin. He was out cold and in need of urgent medical attention. One of the shop staff brought out a cushion, which Neal placed beneath Hannigan's head. Gorse, although conscious, was in no fit state to attempt an escape. To make doubly certain, Neal cuffed him to an undamaged lamp post, the nearby onlookers giving the crook a wide berth.

Mal Brady dealt with any oncoming traffic, directing it round the stricken getaway car, whose ruptured engine was hissing sinisterly, while Neal returned to the bank to tell everyone inside that the situation was under control but to stay put for the time being. He returned the stolen money to the branch manager and checked on the condition of the elderly guard.

The manager informed him that the police and an ambulance were on their way. The guard had been bundled aside and clubbed with the butt of Eddie Hannigan's gun. He was conscious but needed to be checked out.

Within minutes, an ambulance had arrived alongside reinforcements from the station in the persons of Tom Wrightson and PCs Hodgson and Palgrave. Hannigan's skull had been fractured as a result of his head making violent contact with the pavement when Mal Brady had ploughed into him. Mal wasn't the tallest but carried some bulk, mainly, Neal felt, due to the consumption of illicit snacks and breakfasts while out on inquiries. But Neal wasn't going to complain.

Hannigan was likely to be out of circulation for a while and would be transferred from the Radcliffe Infirmary to a prison hospital as soon as it could be safely done. Tom sent Jon Palgrave to the hospital with the ambulance to report back on progress.

As they transferred Kelvin Gorse into the back of the squad car, Neal gave Tom a verbal account of what had happened, knowing he'd anyway be writing it up in a report once he was back at the station. Tom had taken charge of Hannigan's gun. "Always was a ruddy hothead," was his comment. "Real, live ammo in there, lad. And he wouldn't have held back from using it, even though he might have ended up swinging for it. You can tell your young missus, but make sure she's sitting down when you do."

While they were speaking, Paul Hodgson was moving the crowd on. Tom had called for a breakdown truck, and on its arrival, Mal Brady oversaw the removal of the robbers' car.

"Hey, Sergeant!" one of the departing onlookers called out to Tom. "Reckon those two plainclothes boys should get a medal for what they did today!"

"Likely they will, from what I've been told," Tom called back. He turned to Neal. "Blimey, lad, I reckon you cut it a bit fine, but well done. There's bound to be a commendation for the pair of you."

"Certainly there should be for Mal," Neal said. "I'd have been a goner but for him."

Tom grinned. "Wonders will never cease. But I'll admit the lad's got more about him than he lets on." He went on to say that he and Paul would take Gorse back to the cells for Neal and Brady to interview later. "Best get yourselves back there, too, Gally, and have a sit down and a couple of mugs of strong tea."

Leaving the clearing up in Tom's capable hands, Neal and Mal walked back to where they'd left the car. It was the first opportunity Neal had had to thank his colleague for his prompt action earlier.

"You saved my life back there, Mal. I promise you I shan't forget that in a hurry."

He offered a hand, which Mal shook, looking embarrassed and a little dazed. "You'd have done the same for me, Gally. For any of us."

Tom must have called ahead to the station, because they walked in to be greeted by a welcoming committee of Phil Winter, Sally Dakers, Pam and Yvonne, among others. Yvonne fetched tea and biscuits, while Winter offered his sincere congratulations to both men, informing them that he'd be reporting on their exploits to Don Pilling. Neal felt this was decent of him, particularly as Sally told him later that Winter had not long come back from a meeting with the DCI where, from what she'd gathered, he'd been severely hauled over the coals for the botched attempt to rescue Cressida Horwood the previous evening. Apparently, the girl's father had made his feelings plain to the ACC, and the blame had been duly passed down the line. Neal hoped Pilling wouldn't have a relapse when he heard of Mal Brady's heroism.

Naturally, Larry Rackham had got wind of the incident and turned up at the station as bold as brass. "OUT!" Phil Winter had thundered, his normally pale features turning bright red. "I warned you when you came to see me earlier that you're no longer welcome here. Set foot in my station again, and I'll have you arrested."

He did, however, relent, explaining that he'd deliver a statement to the press outside the station at 5pm. Neal wondered if he'd heard a rumour of TV cameras being present.

*

Meanwhile, under duress from his niece, Lambert Wilkie was pushing his ancient Land Rover to the limit and praying that he wouldn't get pulled over for speeding. Jill had been on tenterhooks throughout the journey, expressing displeasure in several unladylike terms when they'd been held up by traffic lights on Headington Hill and unhurrying pedestrians at a zebra crossing in St Clements. Before long, however, they were racing down St Aldate's and, at Jill's instruction, Wilkie was turning into the yard outside the station.

Jill was out of the Land Rover before he'd brought it to a halt, not pausing to close the passenger door in her haste. She dashed inside, halted at the front desk by Tom Wrightson's reassuring grin.

"He's in his office, lass, so along you go. Difference is, he's everybody's hero now, not just yours."

Jill, breathless, smiled her gratitude, hurried along the corridor and burst in to find Neal surrounded by Mal Brady, Sally Dakers and Paul Hodgson.

On seeing her, Neal rose from his seat, almost to be knocked back into it as she flew into his arms.

"Oh, Neal darling, thank God you're alright. Uncle Lam called in. He said there'd been a – a shooting?"

He whisked her off her feet, speechless through the force of her welcoming embrace and kiss. He stood holding her tightly, clutching her head against his chest.

"And Sergeant Wrightson said you were a hero." Jill gasped out the words, her hair awry, face beetroot red and spectacle lenses opaque with steam. "Oh, but thank God, thank God you're safe!"

"I don't see myself as much of a hero," Neal remarked, as soon as he was able to get a word in edgeways. "Not compared to Mal. He's the real hero. He saved my life."

"Mal did?" Jill's voice betrayed a hint of disbelief.

"He most certainly did." Neal didn't elaborate, deciding to do so later, knowing that Jill, in her customary spirit of thoroughness, would want to hear chapter and verse. And as Tom had recommended earlier, he'd make sure she was sitting down when he did, with just the two of them present and a glass of scotch in their hands.

But for now, Jill took Neal at his word, released her grip on him and turned to where Mal was standing, trying to look unobtrusive.

Jill walked over and planted a huge kiss on his stubbly cheek. "I really don't know how to thank you, Mal," she said. "But, well – *thank you*."

"Blimey, love." Mal looked stunned. "If that's the reaction I'm likely to get, I don't mind saving his life every day."

Sensing they were surplus to requirements, Sally signalled to Paul and Mal that they should leave the couple alone for a while. She ushered them out of the office and pulled the door up softly behind them.

Colonel Wilkie had just walked into the station and saw the office door closing. He grinned, as Tom greeted him with raised eyebrows.

"Looks as if I may be waiting here a while, as that seems to be the way of it," Wilkie remarked casually. "Follow rugger, do you, Sergeant? Which way d'you think the Varsity match will go this year?"

Later that afternoon, Neal and Mal Brady interviewed a downcast Kelvin Gorse. He'd only come out of prison the previous week and would shortly be heading back inside.

"It was Eddie's idea," he groaned. "All he asked was for me to be the wheel man. See, I needed the dosh so's I could get away from ruddy Oxford."

"That's soon going to be happening anyway," Mal murmured unsympathetically.

Neal questioned Gorse as to where he'd been since leaving prison, and it transpired that he'd been dropping in on several of his relatives, ending up with Cousin Eddie and his mum. Neal made a mental note of the Gorse clan's lack of co-operation. He and Brady had called on most of them over the past couple of days, and no-one had given them a sniff of where Kelvin might have been holed up. Neal was having a private wager with himself that Gorse hadn't been responsible for Jerry Rudd's death. Even so, he was bound to question him about it, and he and Brady did so at length.

"First I knew," Kelvin said, "was when I read about it in the *Mail* the other day. Couldn't have happened to a more deserving bloke. Otherwise, I might have gone after him and given him a kicking, 'cause I know for sure he grassed on me over that Summertown job I got sent down for. But no, Mr Gallian, nothing to do with me, I swear. I'd never have topped him. I was with one or other of that list of people I just given you. You can check it out."

"Oh, don't worry, Kelvin," Neal replied. "We shall. But we'll also be making sure you didn't send one of your family in his direction."

"But I didn't, I promise you," Gorse whined. "Cross my heart, 'cause I'd swing for it too, wouldn't I, if I had? And it sure as hell wouldn't be worth swinging for a little rat like Jerry Rudd."

Neal grinned tightly. *Another fitting epitaph.*

*

Earlier, Neal had sent Jill back to the flat with her uncle, assuring her that, once he'd interviewed Kelvin Gorse, he'd tie up a few more ends and hopefully be home at a reasonable hour. There'd been tears to be stemmed as Jill had blamed herself for insisting he call into a bank to cash a cheque, but his response was that although he'd walked into a bank many times during his adult life, that day had been the first occasion he'd entered one which was in the process of being robbed. The money issue was finally settled when Jill said she'd cash the cheque that afternoon in the city centre, in the company of her uncle.

Finally, with Jill and Wilkie gone, Gorse interviewed and shut away in his cell, and Mal being cosseted by the canteen ladies, Neal had the chance to sit and reflect on what had happened that morning and put it down in a report.

Of all the images which had flashed across his mind as he'd stood rooted to the spot, transfixed by the sight of the gun in Eddie Hannigan's hand, Jill's had been the most vibrant. But he was startled by one face which he'd neither expected nor wished to be there: that of Helen Holt.

Neal had never told Jill of his affair with Helen. It had happened two years before he'd even met her. Jill, in her innocence, had always been candid with him, and yet he'd so far felt unable to share his secret with her.

It wasn't that he harboured any feelings of rekindling that relationship with Helen. She'd returned briefly to Oxford several months back and had sought him out, in her words to catch up and apologize for having walked out on him as he'd lain helpless in his hospital bed, when she'd roundly blamed him for the fact that her husband was dead and Neal had survived.

At the time, he'd been devastated by her anger, her desertion. And when, finally, she'd returned, perhaps seeking a way back into his life, Neal had let her down as gently as he'd been able. In any case, he was engaged to Jill by then, and while he was glad, relieved, that he now had Helen's apology and forgiveness, she no longer meant anything to him, apart from the fact that he'd still regard her as a friend.

And he knew he'd have to tell Jill about that episode from his past before long. His conscience would demand it. He didn't want there to be any secrets between them and would seek the right moment.

But there'd been one image which, to his amazement, had been missing as he'd stared down the barrel of the gun.

The Face.

For so long, there'd hardly been a day when he'd not been haunted by the memory of the man, pale and terrified, staring back through the warehouse window almost three years previously, seconds before the first boom of the gun which had killed Clyde, the next which had put him out of action and plunged him into the pit of despair.

Neal had encountered the Face again back in March, when the man had narrowly slipped through his fingers, having killed once again – killed through fear of discovery, as he firmly believed.

DCI Pilling had taken Neal off the case before it could turn once more into an obsession, and the subsequent investigation had petered out dispiritedly. They'd been unable to trace the man or discover anything, even the smallest detail, about him.

Neal supposed he hadn't given the matter much thought since then. The DCI had forbidden it, and his word was law. Besides, the debt Neal owed his boss was too great that he should go against his word. Other investigations had come along, there'd been preparations for the wedding, the wedding itself, and above all else Jill, whose love in the past year and three months had proved the constant factor, the force which drove him on.

As they sat together at home that evening, and he gave Jill the full details of what had happened at the bank that morning, he could tell that she didn't want to dwell on those events. Purposeful as ever, Jill wanted them both to move on.

To that end, she told him about Anne Barcham, how she'd taken the unfortunate woman's plight to heart, and how she wondered if anything could be done to find out whether Anne's daughter might still be alive.

Glad for the distraction, Neal promised to look into the story's background and perhaps, when he had more time on his hands, check in Records and ask Tom Wrightson for any details he might recall.

17

While Neal and Mal were busy interviewing Kelvin Gorse, Sally Dakers stepped out of the office to check a few details with Tom Wrightson on a minor matter which had landed on her desk. As they stood with their heads bent over the paperwork, the outer door sprang open and, preceded by a blast of cold November air, an irate figure stalked in. Sally's heart sank as she recognized Dalton Horwood, who was clearly in no mood for exchanging pleasantries.

"Where's DI Winter? I demand to see him now!" His fist crashed down on the desk, as his booming voice echoed down the corridor. Sally noticed that he clutched a sheet of paper in his free hand. Tom's indignant stare, normally enough to freeze anyone in their tracks, didn't register with him at all.

She was spared from making a reply as Phil Winter emerged from his office. He'd have had to have been sound asleep not to have heard the MP's rageful tones.

"I'm here, Mr Horwood. How can I help?"

Sally was no great fan of Winter, but she admired his dignity and professionalism. He must have felt as jittery inside as she did, witnessing the pompous Horwood so obviously on the warpath, but he remained polite and respectful in the face of the MP's boiling anger.

Horwood's face was dangerously suffused, and Sally wondered how regularly he allowed his doctor to check him out. An audience had gathered: Yvonne, Pam, Paul and several others. Behind Horwood's back, Tom gestured to them all to return to what they'd been doing.

The MP brandished the sheet of paper at Winter as he approached, and Sally noticed the tell-tale capital letters cut from a newspaper and pasted onto it.

"A brick was thrown through my study window not an hour ago," he thundered. "This was tied to it. And now I have the expense of replacing the glass *and* a demand for *seven* thousand pounds, thanks to your incompetence in allowing that idiot of a journalist to wreck last night's rendezvous."

Winter remained calm. "Perhaps we'll head along to my office to discuss the matter, sir?"

"Humph! Very well." Horwood followed him down to the office with bad grace. Sally felt he scarcely deserved the DI's respect, also that Horwood wouldn't be able to count on many votes from her colleagues when the next election came around – and it was generally felt, given the new Labour government's tiny majority, that one might not be long in coming.

She was still at the front desk when Horwood came out. He'd been in there for barely ten minutes. "Remember, Winter, I'm counting on you," was his parting threat, as he swept past the desk and out to his car without according anyone else a word or a glance.

Phil Winter appeared in his doorway, pale but collected, and called Sally in. Once he'd spoken to her, she returned to Neal's office to find him back from his interview with Gorse. He asked what the row had been about earlier, and she told him.

"So, you're on again for tonight?"

"Yes. Mr Horwood just wants the DI and myself present. He doesn't want any sort of trap set for the kidnappers, but for us to allow him simply to hand over the money and get his daughter safely back. Poor girl. It's been over three days now. Hard to imagine how she must be feeling."

"Where are you meeting?"

"Hopford Halt? I've no idea where it is. The DI says he knows it."

"A small station on a disused branch line – once again in the middle of nowhere. They've chosen well and must know the area."

"Let's hope nothing goes wrong this time. The DI's trying to track them down using two of the WPCs to check on all motorbikes with sidecars registered in the county."

Neal whistled. "That's some task, and it'll take some time."

"I dare say it will," Sally replied. "But it's the only lead we've got."

*

Any hopes Neal might have had of getting away on time that afternoon were scuppered when Yvonne Begley came up with the details of the car which had been spotted in Jericho on the night of Jerry Rudd's murder and in Botley the previous night. It was a Ford Cortina registered to a Robert Sanderson with an address in Witney, about twelve miles away. He sent a squad car to bring Sanderson in, the officers catching him just as he was walking back to his digs from where he'd parked his car.

Sanderson's landlady, a substantial, middle-aged matron, wasn't too happy about the appearance of two uniformed policemen appearing on her doorstep – what *would* the neighbours think? – and she argued that her lodger was a polite, well brought-up young man who couldn't possibly have done anything to break the law. And furthermore, his tea would be ruined.

Bob Sanderson himself didn't make an issue of Jon Palgrave's request to accompany them to Oxford. He was pale and subdued and, the young PC reported to Neal, it seemed almost as if he'd been expecting them to call.

Neal introduced himself and Mal and led Sanderson along to the interview room. He was younger than Neal had anticipated, mid-twenties, a tall, good-looking, fair-haired man in a grey suit, slightly rumpled after what Neal assumed had been a long day at work. As he invited Sanderson to sit, Neal could tell he was nervous. What had he got to hide?

Neal and Mal sat across the table from Sanderson, and Neal pointed out that they had some questions for him with regard to an incident in Jericho the Sunday night just past.

"I believe you own a car, Mr Sanderson? A white Ford Cortina, registration number PBL 953?"

"Yes, that's mine." Sanderson looked puzzled. "But it's okay, because I've got it back now."

Neal frowned. "Got it back? I didn't realize you'd been without it." He glanced at Brady, who shrugged.

"Yes. It must have been stolen on Sunday night."

The look on Mal's face suggested that that seemed rather convenient.

"Then clearly it can't have been missing for very long?"

Sanderson fidgeted in his seat, embarrassed. "Um, no. I park it in a yard behind a pub in my street, you see. When I went there to drive it to my first appointment on Monday morning, it had gone."

"You reported it missing?"

"Yes, I went round to Witney police station right away. I returned to my digs and was about to phone through to cancel my appointments when they called to say they'd found it, parked down a lane at the bottom of my street."

"Any damage?" Mal didn't bother to mask his disbelief.

Bob Sanderson looked mystified. "No. Fortunately, no real damage at all."

Neal was inclined to agree with his colleague: it seemed too convenient. He pressed on. "You hadn't lent the car to anyone?"

"I'm not allowed to. It's a company car."

"Ah, right. So, which company do you work for, Mr Sanderson?"

"X-Pressive Stationery Supplies. We're based in Cheltenham. I'm representative for the South Midlands area?"

Stationery. Rudd had been stabbed with a letter opener, an item which was easily available from any number of stores. Neal could tell that Mal was thinking along the same lines: this looked promising.

"Have you been with them long?" he asked.

"About eighteen months."

"Who do you report to?"

"Mike Braddon. He's the Sales Manager, based at Head Office." Sanderson fished in a pocket and brought out a card, which he handed across to Neal. It listed Braddon's office and Sanderson's home phone numbers.

Neal was aware that Sanderson had started to relax, possibly thinking that his explanation about the stolen car had absolved him. Time to ramp up the pressure.

"So, Mr Sanderson, you got your car back on Monday morning?"

"Yes. Thankfully, I was able to complete my appointments."

"Then you would have had it on Tuesday evening, when one of our constables spotted it in Botley?"

The question had been put casually, but Bob Sanderson's reaction was far from relaxed. His mouth fell open, and he shifted uncomfortably on his chair.

"Been calling on someone, had you?" Mal managed to load his question with a salacious hint, and it did the trick.

"Um, I -er, yes. I was visiting a friend."

"What's the name of this friend?"

A little colour had begun to appear on the young man's cheeks as the interview had gone on, but it had quickly vanished, leaving him once again pale and uncertain.

Neal stepped in, the antidote to Mal's brusqueness. "Mr Sanderson, we've brought you in because this is a very serious matter. Your car was seen parked in Jericho last Sunday night, around the time a man was murdered. His body was found in the canal the following morning."

"But I wasn't there!" Sanderson protested. "I couldn't have been. My car was stolen that night. I reported it the next morning."

"Yes, sir. I don't doubt that you reported it. But we only have your word for it having been stolen."

"But – but I assure you it was," the young man spluttered.

He was about to protest further, but Neal raised a silencing hand to prevent him. "Do you know a man named Jerry Rudd?"

"Rudd? Isn't that the name of the murdered man? The body in the canal? No, no, I swear I'd never heard of him before reading about it in the paper."

"Okay, Mr Sanderson. So, where were you on Sunday night?"

"Just at my digs. On Sundays, Mrs Daines, my landlady, provides a tea – scones and cakes that she's baked. I – I had it with her and her husband. Then we sat and watched television, like we usually do. *Sunday Night at the London Palladium.* Afterwards, I went up to my room and read for a while before going to bed."

"And you didn't go out?"

"I swear I didn't. Not until the following morning when I went round to the yard and found my car gone."

Neal handed Mal the business card. "I take it this is Mrs Daines' number, sir?" Sanderson nodded, yes. "DC Brady's about to give her a ring, just so that we can confirm your alibi for Sunday night."

Mal pushed back his chair and left the room, while Neal sat and waited. He felt sure the landlady would corroborate her lodger's story. But the young man was far from at ease, running a hand over his face, shifting around on his chair and looking anywhere but at Neal.

Within a few minutes, Brady appeared in the doorway, beckoning Neal out into the corridor.

"It all checks out," he said, keeping his voice low. "Mrs Daines reckons she's a light sleeper. The stairs creak, and the front door sticks in this cold weather. She's adamant she'd have heard if he'd gone out at all that night."

Neal nodded his thanks, and the two of them went back into the room and resumed their seats.

Bob Sanderson looked up hopefully.

"Your landlady confirms what you told us," Neal said. He paused, his gaze not leaving the young man's face. He wanted Sanderson to understand that he wasn't off the hook.

"There's something troubling you," Neal went on. "And it's best if you come clean with us. Let me ask you again. Who did you visit in Botley on Tuesday evening? I want a name."

"Oh, dear Lord…" Sanderson leaned forward on to his elbows and covered his face with his hands. "I don't want to make things worse for her. I visited her on Tuesday evening, but I swear to you that neither of us had anything to do with that man's death."

"Her name, please, Mr Sanderson?"

He looked up at last, the picture of a soul in torment.

"Avril. Mrs Avril Walden. She lives at 53, Faversham Close. She's the manageress at Paper, Pen & Ink in the Cornmarket. Her husband doesn't know about – that we're seeing each other. Look, she'll be at home tomorrow – it's her day off. Sh-she'll vouch for me – she knows my car was stolen. Oh, Lord, you think I murdered this man, don't you?"

"I've no proof of that," Neal said. "But we need to look into this further. We'll call on Mrs Walden in the morning. In the meantime, sir, I'd be grateful if you didn't contact her."

"I won't, I promise. But -?" He stared open-mouthed at Neal, then at Mal Brady. "Does this mean you're letting me go?"

Neal grinned. "You're not under arrest, Mr Sanderson. But we'll probably need to speak to you again once we've seen Mrs Walden. If you wait here for a few minutes, I'll get someone to run you back to your digs."

As he left the room, Neal was rather glad that Bob Sanderson had been sitting down, otherwise he felt the young man might have fainted with relief.

18

They took an unmarked car again, dark blue so that it blended with the night. Winter drove, as Sally was unfamiliar with the location. She realized he didn't only know where it was but must have earlier carried out a careful reconnaissance. His thoroughness impressed her, but she understood that he couldn't afford to slip up again, particularly where someone like Dalton Horwood was concerned.

Once again, the lane was narrow and remote. As they passed over the hump of a bridge, Winter pointed out that Hopford Halt lay down beyond it, not that it was possible to see anything, as there was no lighting anywhere around. He parked the car some two hundred yards on and a little way down a rutted track, so that it was hidden from the road. A steady, cold rain was falling as they walked back to the bridge along the verge, feet squelching in the long grass.

The rendezvous had again been arranged for 8pm, so they had more than an hour of waiting to endure. Neither of them spoke. Winter indicated some bushes at the roadside close to the bridge where Sally would wait, while he would make his way down a flight of steps and conceal himself in the shrubbery beyond the platform.

He'd been adamant before they left: they were there to observe, to obtain the registration number of the kidnappers' vehicle and any details they could notice of the men themselves. The overriding aim was to get Cressida Horwood back safely: that was all her father wanted, and he'd made that abundantly clear to Winter that afternoon.

It was essential that nothing went wrong. Sally had learned from Tom Wrightson that Winter had received a tongue-lashing from DCI Pilling earlier that day and suspected that the ACC had come down hard on him, despite the fact that Winter had been his choice. That summed up her idea of the top brass: bask in the glory of success, but be quick to shift any blame elsewhere, keeping your own hands scrupulously clean.

Sally set herself to endure a long wait in the steadily dripping shrubbery. At least she wasn't in the bushes with the DI again, despite the ribbing she'd received earlier from one or two of her colleagues.

Time dragged mournfully by. Sally's first glance at the luminous dial of her watch told her it was seven-fifteen. She'd been waiting twenty minutes, which had seemed like twenty hours. She was in the middle of stifling a sigh, when she heard a rustling in the shrubbery behind her, followed by the soft slap of a footfall.

Sally broke the DI's rule. "Sir?" she whispered. "Is that you?"

Her answer was the sudden prick of something sharp against her neck, and a heavy hand falling on her shoulder. She gasped as a sibilant whisper slid out of the darkness. "Not a sound, sweetheart. Or else…"

Sally realized that the man held a knife, and that it had pierced her skin. She strove to remain calm.

"I know you're a cop," the voice continued. "I seen you out on the road with the other one. Where is he?"

She fought to form and then force out the words: they seemed to stick in her throat. "He – he's down on the platform."

Her reward was a nasty, guttural chuckle. "Sounds good. Any more of you around? Lie to me, sweetheart, and I'll cut you. I mean it."

She was sure he did. "No-one."

"Okay. So, we wait here, and you keep your mouth shut. Tight shut, right? Remember, I got this." He laid the flat of the cold blade against her cheek. "Don't breathe a word."

Sally tried to summon up some resilience, reflecting on the bravery of DS Gallian and DC Brady that morning. She told herself that this was a completely different situation, that there must be no heroics with the man pressing up close behind her and the knife so perilously adjacent. She was feeling several stages away from any heroism, fighting to gather her wits, to remain focused, above all not to faint…

Perversely, the hectoring tones of her old Games mistress came flying back to her. *"Put some beef into it, Dakers. Look at the size of you."* Sally could almost hear her now. *"Some policewoman you are…"* But some policewoman she intended to remain. Blowed if she was going to get herself killed just to satisfy the death-or-glory principles of Bertha 'Bully' Bulstrode.

She felt clammy all over, felt, too, as if she'd been waiting there for days, if she'd be able to move at all when the time came. But at last, she heard the approaching sound of a powerful vehicle: Horwood's Land Rover, she felt sure.

So did her unwelcome companion, reaching forward to part the branches as headlights fanned out across the narrow road. The Land Rover drew to a halt just past the bridge, a door opened, and well-shod feet hit the ground. Beyond the headlights, Sally made out Dalton Horwood's figure, the small suitcase held at his side. He was looking around nervously, casting wild glances in every direction.

"Winter? Are you here?"

The voice leaked out of the darkness, squeaky and unmanned, indistinguishable from the bawling tones they'd had no trouble hearing back at the nick that afternoon.

The question was answered by a blast of light and the roar of a motorbike from beyond the bridge. Horwood was transfixed in the glare, spinning round startled before stepping back against the side of his vehicle.

The knife was snatched away from where it had rested against Sally's neck. The man waved it at her threateningly. "Stay there," he growled and shouldered his way through the shrubbery and out on to the road. She had a glimpse of a hooded, dark-clad figure, as he moved past the Land Rover's headlights.

The motorbike and sidecar, meanwhile, had come to a halt close to where Horwood was standing, the engine still running and its rider sitting astride his machine with his hands on the handlebars, now and again revving the engine.

The first man had tucked his knife into a sheath around his waist. He strode past the paralysed MP, lifted the hood of the sidecar and dragged out a slight, struggling figure.

"Money all there, mush?" he rapped.

Horwood held out the suitcase at arm's length. "Yes. It – it's all here."

"Worse for you if it isn't. Here – take her." He propelled the girl towards her father, snatched the case and pitched it into the sidecar, rammed down the hood and climbed onto the pillion seat.

Horwood held out his arms, and the girl almost tripped headlong into his embrace.

"*Cressida! Oh, darling!*"

"*Daddy!*"

Their words were drowned as the rider opened the throttle, and the motorbike tore past them. At the same time, Sally tumbled into the road, peering after it, but the rear numberplate had been slathered with mud and was impossible to read. Sally stood trembling, gazing after it, as she felt the warm wriggle of blood on her neck. She took a handkerchief from her pocket and dabbed at the wound, knowing that it was only slight and that, above all else, Cressida Horwood was safe.

Father and daughter were welded together in a bear hug, the girl weeping tears of relief, and the man deeply emotional, murmuring over and over as he nuzzled her hair, "Oh, my darling girl. You're safe, safe. Thank God."

Sally, looking on, the tiny handkerchief pressed tightly against her neck, felt that the MP's reaction somewhat redeemed him in her view, witnessing his obvious relief and the love which dwelt even in his politician's heart.

She turned as a frazzled-looking Winter appeared at the top of the steps beside the bridge, his anxious gaze switching from the entwined Horwoods to his WDC. "They said to rendezvous on the platform," he complained peevishly.

"They were ahead of us anyway, sir," Sally replied levelly. "They knew the territory."

"You think they're local to this part of the county?" Winter asked, probably, Sally reflected, the first time he'd sought her opinion about anything.

"Almost certainly, I'd say, sir."

"Hhmm, well, at least that's something." He peered at her closely. "Dakers, are you hurt?"

Sally told him what had happened: the kidnappers had been waiting for her, how long they'd been there she couldn't tell, and she'd been powerless to say or do anything with the knife held in such close proximity. Fortunately, the wound was very slight, and the bleeding had practically stopped.

As Winter took this on board, tut-tutting sympathetically, Sally approached the Horwoods, suddenly wondering what Cressida must have gone through and wanting to calm her, at the same time attempting to calm her still trembling self.

Dalton Horwood looked up as she drew near.

"Mr Horwood, would you like me to sit with Cressida while you drive us back?" she asked.

The MP stared at her blankly, as if not quite sure why Sally was there. "Why, -er, yes," he replied, sounding taken aback. "Yes. Th -thank you."

Winter had followed Sally over and threw her a tight smile and nod of approbation. "I'll follow on behind, Mr Horwood."

That merited a grunt from the MP, as he passed his daughter over into Sally's care. Winter grinned lamely and headed off down the lane to retrieve his car.

"I'm sorry, Daddy," the girl sobbed. "You paid money to get me back. I heard them talking about it. Was it a lot of money?"

"The money doesn't matter, darling," Horwood replied, and Sally was close enough to witness the real tenderness in his expression. "You're back with us and safe. That's all that matters."

He planted a kiss on her forehead, nodded at Sally and got into the Land Rover, while she took Cressida by the arm and ushered her into the back seat, climbing in alongside her.

The girl looked a mess: face grubby, clothes rumpled, and blonde hair matted and tangled. "They didn't hurt you, did they?" Sally had a sudden, disturbing vision of a pretty girl alone with two burly men, full of menace. Cressida was clearly distraught, more tears falling, and Sally put an arm around her and cuddled her tightly.

"No, th-they didn't hurt me," the girl mumbled. "Just kept me locked up. I was so – so *frightened*."

Sally could understand her distress. It was laughable to think that the kidnapping might have been a deliberate ploy on Cressida's part. If she was putting on an act, she deserved to be on the West End stage.

As they turned through the gates of Farway House, the Land Rover's headlights picked out Marjorie Horwood and Dennis Nolan waiting expectantly beside the open front door. They came running up as Horwood eased to a halt, and Sally helped the girl out of her seat. As her feet hit the ground, she staggered a little, but Sally managed to bear her up long enough for her to be swallowed into the fond embraces of her mother and boyfriend. Both Cressida and Marjorie were in tears, and Dennis Nolan choked with emotion. "Oh, Cress, honey, I was so scared for you. I thought – oh, dear God, I thought I'd never see you again."

Sally and Horwood stood to one side, the MP looking on with a weary smile, although Sally felt he still harboured a distrust of Nolan. Again, if the boy was acting, it was a superb performance.

Winter had rolled the police car to an unobtrusive halt behind everyone. He got out and walked over to join Sally and Horwood.

"We'll call back in the morning, sir," he advised the MP respectfully. "Once your daughter's rested, we can discover what she might be able to tell us about the kidnappers and her time as their prisoner."

Horwood accorded him a distracted nod. "Yes, yes, of course. But the main thing is, she's safe. Thank you, Winter."

The DI was dismissed and knew it. He nodded to Sally, and they turned and walked back towards the car.

"WDC Dakers!" They both turned as Dennis Nolan came running up to Sally. His face no longer looked drawn but seemed to shine with relief.

"I just wanted to thank you – for all you've done – your support. Oh, and you too, Inspector." He was racing back to join the others before Sally could form a reply.

Winter had walked on to reach the car and, as she joined him, Sally felt he seemed downcast. "Let's hope Cressida can give us a lead of some sort tomorrow, Dakers," he said. Then he seemed to brighten a little. "Oh, and well done tonight, by the way. You were very brave. Must say it seems to be a feature of my team."

Sally thanked him as they got into the car. It seemed rather typical of her temporary boss that he should manage to salvage a little reflected glory for himself.

19

The next morning, before setting out to call on Avril Walden, Neal went along to Phil Winter's office to update him on progress in their search for Jerry Rudd's killer. Winter heard him out, nodding along, but Neal could tell he was distracted, having his hands full with trying to track down Cressida Horwood's kidnappers. Now the girl was safely back, he guessed her father would be demanding results – soon, and in no uncertain terms.

Winter's opinion, as Neal might have guessed, was that he should have arrested Bob Sanderson on suspicion of murder. Neal had his reply ready: no tangible proof plus, as investigating officer, he wasn't convinced that Sanderson was their man.

However, the DI wasn't going to argue the point. "I'm sure you know what you're doing, Neal. Just keep me posted, won't you?"

It was just after nine when Neal and Mal Brady knocked on the Waldens' front door. Their front garden was small but reasonably tidy, as if whoever looked after it did the bare minimum to keep it up to scratch.

There was no immediate reply, so Neal knocked again, noticing the blurred outline of someone appearing in the hallway. The door opened to reveal an attractive blonde in her thirties, a little on the plump side although still managing to look appealing in housecoat and slippers. Neal showed his warrant card and introduced himself and Brady. Avril Walden stood aside to let them in.

Neal's next words were drowned out by a volley of curses and the thundering of heavy feet from above.

"Avril! What the hell's going on? I'm trying to sleep up here."

A large, ungainly man in striped pyjamas appeared on the stairs, a portrait of tousled rage. Avril Walden looked up apologetically. "Sorry, Neville." She turned to Neal. "My husband's not long back from his night shift, Sergeant."

"Sorry to have disturbed you, Mr Walden," Neal called up. "Oxford CID. We just need a few words with your wife."

The man's full lips compressed in a nasty smirk. "Dear, oh dear, Avril. What *have* you been up to?"

But the smirk faded as he caught Mal Brady peering up at him. "Er, sorry. Bit grumpy after a long shift. I'll get back to bed."

"Apologies again for disturbing you," Neal called after him, with Brady adding, "We promise to keep our voices down." But Walden was already plodding back up the stairs. Moments later, a door closed behind him.

"Let's talk in the kitchen," Avril suggested. She was looking pale and anxious as she lowered her voice. "I can guess why you're here."

She led them into a neatly kept square kitchen, gleaming black-and-white chequered linoleum floor, cooker, fridge, washing machine and a small table with a chair at each end. Avril pointed the detectives to the chairs and pulled up a kitchen stool for herself.

Unexpectedly, Mal Brady was first to speak, in his usual matey tone. "Your husband up at the works, Mrs Walden?"

Avril smiled thinly. "Yes. He used to work as a garage mechanic, but it's better money up there."

"He's got to have a big interest in cars, then?"

"Oh, him and cars! Yes, more than anything else. He's always tinkering around. He and his friend often buy one cheap to do up and sell on."

"Ah, right."

Neal threw Mal a quizzical look, and he winked in response. Avril had turned away to lift a teapot from its stand. "Like a cup?" she asked. "I've just made it."

Both men said yes, and Avril took extra cups and saucers from the cupboard above where she stood and poured the tea. Neal noticed her hands shaking slightly as she did so.

He waited until she'd brought the tea over and had perched on the stool, hands round her cup, as if seeking comfort from its warmth.

"Mrs Walden, are you acquainted with Robert Sanderson?"

She'd known the question was coming, but even so couldn't prevent her face registering a pained expression. Her reply was to slip down off her stool, go to the kitchen door, open it and take a step into the hallway to cautiously check the stairs. She returned, closed the door softly and tried to compose herself.

"Yes," she said quietly. "Bob's a friend of mine."

Neal flicked a wary glance at Brady, worried that he might make some embarrassing quip. But he maintained a bland expression, his gaze on Avril's face: he was learning.

"We're investigating a murder, Mrs Walden," Neal went on. "A man's body was found in the canal in Jericho early on Monday morning. A witness had noticed a parked car in the adjacent street around the time the murder was committed. Inquiries established that it didn't belong to a resident. The car was traced to Mr Sanderson, and the victim had been stabbed with a letter opener, a type featured in the catalogue of X-Pressive Stationery Supplies – the company for which, as you'll be aware, Mr Sanderson works."

Avril Walden had begun to shake her head long before Neal had finished speaking. "But Bob couldn't have been there," she protested. "His car was stolen that evening – surely, he's told you that?"

"Mr Sanderson *reported* it stolen," Neal corrected. "It was found the next morning, not far from where he'd parked it. There was no damage: it hadn't been broken into."

"If Bob says it was stolen, then I believe him," Avril hit back stubbornly. "I can assure you, Sergeant, that he didn't kill anyone. We both read about the murder in the *Oxford Mail,* and neither of us recognized the man's name."

"Jerry Rudd was well known to us," Neal said, carefully watching Avril's expression as he described the man in life. "He was a criminal through and through, but slippery. Not a lot that he wasn't into. But you knew him, didn't you, Mrs Walden, even if you didn't know his name?"

Avril sighed and cleared her throat. When she spoke, it was in a low, level voice, and Neal could tell the effort she made was costing her dear.

"I'm in an unhappy marriage, Sergeant Gallian," she said. "It's cost me close on ten years of my life, and I've known it for at least eight of those. I manage the stationery store, Paper, Pen & Ink, in the city centre. Since the summer, I've become friendly with Bob Sanderson, the new area rep for X-P, and in that time, we've moved some way beyond friendship. Bob's a really gentle soul. I can tell he cares for me, and for once in my life I feel valued.

"A month ago, I left the shop in the evening and queued in Queen Street for a bus home. I noticed a man leering at me. It was the man you described, the murdered man, Rudd, although I didn't learn his name until I read about his death in the paper. He must have followed me home, because I'd not been indoors two minutes when a note dropped through the letter box. It was a blackmail demand: £200, or he'd tell my husband about my friendship with Bob and also inform Bob's company.

"I've no idea how Rudd could have known about us, but I knew I'd simply fall apart if I couldn't see Bob again. I had a few savings, scraped together the money and paid up. Not long after, Rudd phoned me late one evening when my husband was at work. He asked for more money, but I couldn't pay. I was so miserable. Neville – my husband – never noticed, but Bob did. I didn't want to tell him, but he kept pressing me about it, and in the end, I broke down and told him."

"What was his reaction?"

"He flew into a rage. It shocked me. He wanted to come with me the next time – I'd been instructed to leave the money behind a gravestone in Osney churchyard. He intended to lie in wait for the blackmailer and sort him out. But, Sergeant Gallian, Bob was just shocked and anxious like me, fearing the end of our friendship. I *swear* he'd never have murdered Rudd or anyone."

"So, did Mr Sanderson come with you to meet Rudd?"

"No, he never did. You see, I never went back to the churchyard. I simply hadn't got the further £200 he'd demanded. I – I just thought if I kept quiet, he might get fed up and go away." She chuckled mirthlessly, almost a cough. "And, of course, in a sense he did. Sergeant Gallian, please tell me what will happen now?"

Neal could see that the woman was distraught, and he resolved to let her down as lightly as he could.

"DC Brady and I need to look more closely into this," he said. "It's very likely we shall need to speak to both you and Mr Sanderson again. It'd probably be for the best if you don't contact him for the time being. We'll keep you in touch with what's happening."

He didn't think his words had given her much relief, but she smiled and thanked him, came with them to the door to see them out.

"She's bound to phone him, Gally," Mal said, as they walked back to the car. "Particularly once laughing boy's safely back at work."

"I'm sure she will, Mal. But I don't think it can do much harm. By the way, do you know the husband? He looked a bit startled, as if he recognized you, although I'm sure you have that effect on everyone."

"Oh, very funny. But yes, you're right. I recognized him too. He and his mate tried to sell me a car in a pub a couple of weekends ago. Didn't know the pair of them from Adam, but up they came to me, all matey like. "Hey, pal, why don't we refresh that pint for you, while we have a little chat?" Well, I never say no to a free beer, Gally, but I reckoned something wasn't quite right."

"What were they offering?"

"A Morris Minor. Gave me all the details. They weren't asking a bad price, but I put them off. Hadn't got the money for a start. They moved on quickly to buttonhole somebody else. I put it down to the fact that I didn't like them – not the kind of blokes I'd want to be mates with. And seeing our pal's reaction this morning, I wouldn't mind betting they were dodgy."

"I'd say you were right, Mal. Keep a lookout for them when you're out and about. We've got a name: Neville Walden. And keep me posted."

"Will do. But what about Sanderson? Reckon we should arrest him?"

"Dare say the DI would like that. But I've already given him my take on it."

Mal gave him a long, searching look. "You're not certain it's that simple, are you, Gally?"

"No, Mal, I'm not. Unless the fair Avril and her beau are winding us up – and I don't think they are – something's not sitting right. Someone was going to do something permanent to Jerry Rudd one day. He was a villain through and through, and even the villains didn't like him. What puzzles me is how he got hold of the information he used to blackmail Avril Walden? Both she and Sanderson swear they've never come across him. There must be a third party involved. And then there's Sanderson's car. Let's assume it was stolen, and that the murderer stole it. Then it has to be someone Sanderson knows. But who?"

"Then what you're saying is that Sanderson's off the hook?"

"Not entirely. But for what it's worth, I don't think he's our man."

20

Phil Winter and Sally Dakers drove out to Farway House the next morning. Marjorie Horwood must have been looking out for them, for she was at the door to welcome them in as they drew up. She led them through to the room to which she'd taken Sally the other day, where her daughter was waiting.

Cressida appeared both refreshed after a night's sleep and relieved to be at home and safe. She looked demure in a crisp blouse and plain grey skirt, her newly washed and untangled blonde hair shining and flowing down over her shoulders. She greeted them with a smile and shy words of thanks.

The moment was curtailed as her father strode in, immaculately suited and in a brisk, businesslike mood. The confidence which seemed to have deserted him the previous evening was back. "Right, Winter. You'd better set about tracking down these scoundrels and retrieving my money. How do you propose to go about it?"

"I've already set inquiries in motion, sir." Sally was glad to hear a little asperity in Winter's tone. "Our main aim, as we'd agreed, was to get Miss Horwood back safely."

"Yes, yes. And that's been successfully achieved. I'm due at the house next week for some important debates. It'd be good to get this business cleared up by the weekend, as I shall be travelling up to London late on Sunday afternoon."

Sally was sure Winter felt as exasperated as she did in the MP's hectoring presence. But the DI was spared a reply, as a tentative knock brought Mrs Davis into the room.

"I do apologize for interrupting, sir, but your agent's on the telephone. He says it's urgent."

"Ah, right. Thank you, Davis. Excuse me, Winter, but I'd better take this." With a parting harrumph, Horwood strode out of the room. Once he'd gone, the atmosphere felt more relaxed, and Marjorie Horwood took charge, pointing the detectives to seats.

"Mr Nolan not with you this morning?" Winter asked.

"Denny said he'd call by later." It was Cressida who answered. "He gave me a bell earlier to say he was dropping in on Finlay first to tell him the news."

The girl seemed to have taken a shine to Sally, probably owing to the latter taking her under her wing immediately following her ordeal, and her smiles and words of gratitude had been aimed in her direction rather than towards the DI. Winter, to his credit, had noticed this and nodded for Sally to take the lead with the questioning.

"Miss Horwood," Sally began with a reassuring smile.

"Cressida." The girl beamed back at her.

"Cressida, Mr Winter and I need to ask you a few questions to help us identify your abductors. Can you give us any details about the place where they held you?"

The girl's brow furrowed in thought. "I saw nothing of the outside of the place where they took me. I was unconscious when they carried me away – I suppose I must have fainted. When I came to, I was in a small room. There was a bed, a sideboard, a jug and ewer. Oh, and a bucket for me to - it was covered with a cloth. It was cold in the room. I think it might have been an old house."

"Did they bring you food? Did you see anyone there?"

"One of the men brought it. A big man, but he kept his face hidden, and the blinds were drawn – old blackout blinds, so it was always dark in the room. And he locked the door whenever he went out."

"What sounds did you hear, Cressida? And did anyone mention any names?"

"It was mainly quiet. A few cars went past – and someone on a horse, once. It felt remote. Oh, and I heard a tractor. Although it did sound as if it was some distance away."

"But no names?"

"Only one: 'Ma'. There was a woman in the house. I heard her speaking but couldn't make out the words. She sounded elderly. And a man's voice, quite rough and loud, said something like, "You can't go in there, Ma. She needs to rest – she's not well." He must have meant me."

"Do you remember anything from when they took you out of the room?"

"The man blindfolded me both times. He carried me out and lifted me into the sidecar. He and the other man talked in low voices but never loud enough for me to hear what they were saying."

"Sounds as if Miss Horwood was held at some remote country cottage," Winter summed up needlessly, although Sally could tell from the way he'd been fidgeting that he was aching to have some input. "Possibly near a farm."

She ploughed on, concern in her voice. "Cressida, neither of these men tried to hurt you in any way?"

"Apart from carrying me to and from the house, no-one laid a finger on me."

"And we give thanks for that," Marjorie breathed.

"Cressida, I have to ask this," Sally continued. "But is there anyone you know who might have some sort of grudge against you?"

The girl shook her head. "No-one," she said firmly. "I'm friendly with a group of girls, and we occasionally have our little fallings out, but never anything serious. And I'm on good terms with all Denny's friends."

Winter resumed charge as Dalton Horwood re-entered the room. "Anything useful?" the MP demanded.

"Miss Horwood has been most helpful," the DI replied. "We have a possible lead and will be putting all our energies into following it up." There was a hint of defiance in his words, which Sally silently applauded.

Horwood reached into his jacket pocket for a wallet and extracted a business card, which he handed to Winter. "I need to be in London for most of next week, so here's the telephone number for my flat. You may, of course, also contact me at the House. I shall expect progress reports, Winter. Early evening would be the best time to get in touch."

He'd remained standing in the doorway, as if to indicate that the family had given enough of their time. Winter glanced across at Sally, and she asked Cressida if there was anything else, however small a detail, that she could tell them. The reply was negative, and Winter thanked Cressida and Marjorie and got to his feet. Sally followed suit, also thanking the two women for seeing them.

Horwood accompanied Winter to the door, with Sally following behind. He cast a glance over his shoulder to ensure his womenfolk weren't within earshot and lowered his voice, although Sally had no difficulty overhearing.

"It's my personal belief that Dennis Nolan's not yet out of the wood, Winter," he declared. "I shall expect you to bear that in mind."

"Of course, sir. Rest assured, I shall be speaking to him again." Sally thought it might have been her imagination, but Winter wasn't sounding as subservient to the MP as he'd done on previous occasions. It seemed that, at last, the worm had begun to turn.

They bade Horwood farewell and returned to Oxford. No sooner had they got back to the station than Tom Wrightson informed Winter that DCI Pilling had requested that he go round to see him, as in right away. The ACC had requested an update on the Horwood kidnapping and progress made in tracking down those responsible.

Winter stifled a sigh and went back out again, while Sally took the opportunity to grab a mug of tea and a sandwich and take them back to the office she shared with DS Gallian. Neal was there, head bent over some paperwork, but he took time out to ask how things were progressing. Sally was in the middle of telling him how far they'd got, when Tom Wrightson's head appeared round the door.

"A Mr Nolan and another young man asking to see the DI, Dakers. Something to do with the kidnapping case. Are you okay to see them?"

"Yes, fine, Sarge. I'll come out to the desk."

"Send 'em in here, Tom," Neal offered. "I can make myself scarce for ten minutes."

Sally turned towards him. "I'd rather you stayed, Sarge," she said. "It'd be good to have your input."

"Okay, if you're happy with that."

Tom withdrew and, moments later, ushered in Dennis Nolan and his companion, who turned out to be Finlay Cleave. Sally showed them to chairs and re-introduced Neal, whom they'd both met earlier in the week. Dennis was looking a little flushed and restless, and Sally wondered if this might be important.

"Would this be something to do with the kidnapping, Mr Nolan?" she prompted.

"I've just been to see Fin," Dennis said, a tremor of excitement in his tone. "Just sort of to tell him the good news about Cress. You said about the kidnappers using a motorbike and sidecar?"

"That's right." Sally kept her tone level, at the same time anticipating that they might be about to get somewhere.

Dennis turned to his friend. "Tell them what you just told me, Fin."

"Denny said about the bike," Finlay Cleave said. "See, Mum and Dad were on their way back from Oxford last night, where they'd been to see my Gran. Well, they had an argument with this bike and sidecar coming fast towards them down a single-track lane, and the rider wasn't giving way, travelling at a heck of a lick. He ran them off the road."

"Are they alright?" Sally asked, concerned.

"Just shaken up a bit. Dad managed to swerve into a gateway."

"What time was this?"

"Not sure. But they reckon they must have come away from Gran's at about eight."

The rendezvous at the bridge had been at eight. It seemed to fit.

"Did they by any chance get the registration number?" Sally couldn't keep the expectation out of her voice.

"No." But before she could start to feel disappointed, Finlay added, "But in any case, Dad recognized the driver."

"And who was he?" Sally asked tensely, seeing that Neal was looking on with interest.

"Doug McKerrin."

"Does he live locally?"

"With his mum in a tied cottage a few miles on from us – Hillberry Lane, not far off the Swindon road. He's a labourer at Hillberry Farm."

"Mr Cleave, this could be very useful. I'll pass it on to DI Winter when he gets back."

"It'd be best if neither of you mentioned this to anyone," Neal weighed in. "And by that, I mean anyone at all."

"We'll keep it to ourselves," Dennis Nolan promised. "We want these blokes caught as much as you do. God alone knows what Cress must have gone through."

"I hope she can start to put it behind her now," Sally replied with a smile. "I'm sure you'll do all you can to help her."

"I shan't be letting her out of my sight," Dennis replied resolutely.

Sally felt that Cressida's father might have something to say about that. But she thanked the boys for their input and saw them out of the station. On her return, she looked questioningly at Neal. "Doug McKerrin?"

"Ringing a distant bell, but he's not someone I know personally."

Sally grinned. "Although you're about to say you know someone who does."

"I am. Come on."

He got up and led her out of the office and along to the desk where Tom Wrightson looked up from what he was doing. "What have we got here, then? A deputation?"

"Two detectives seeking information, Tom," Neal said. "Does the name Doug McKerrin mean anything to you?"

Tom hardly had to think. "The only Doug McKerrin I know is a brainless farmhand who comes into town now and again, gets arrested in a drunken brawl and has to be bailed out by his brother."

"His *brother?*"

"Pete McKerrin. Flashy salesman who runs a secondhand car lot up in Cowley. We've never charged him with anything, but I wouldn't put any money on him being straight."

"Top of the form as usual, Tom," Neal enthused. "Thanks. We may just have got a handle on the kidnappers."

"If so, you can buy me a pint," Tom winked.

"I'll buy you one, too," Sally put in.

"I'll hold you to that, lass."

Phil Winter arrived back then. He looked drained, and Sally guessed he'd had a difficult session with the DCI. She thought the news might cheer him up.

"We may have something, sir. Can I fetch you a mug of tea?"

"Oh, thank you, Dakers, if you would. Then join us in my office. Er, Neal? Might we have a word?"

"Of course."

"Don Pilling wants the two of us to liaise more closely on both the Horwood and Rudd cases," Winter explained, once they were seated and out of the way of passing colleagues.

Reading between the lines, Neal guessed that the DCI wanted him in on the search for the kidnappers, and that the ACC was giving Pilling severe earache over the matter.

"Whichever way you want to play it, Phil," he replied diplomatically. "I know a little about the Horwood kidnapping, because I was in the office just now when Dennis Nolan and his friend came along to speak to Dakers. I think it could mean a breakthrough, but I'll let her tell you."

Sally returned with mugs of tea for them all and sat and told the DI what Dennis and Finlay Cleave had told her. Winter brightened as he heard her out.

Winter knew Doug McKerrin, because he'd investigated a charge of assault during his time in Oxford. McKerrin had been given an alibi by his brother, and the charge had been dropped.

"They must be pretty close, then," Neal observed. "Tom seems to think Pete McKerrin often bailed out Doug."

Winter stroked his chin thoughtfully. "Hhmm, could certainly be something there. But where's the connection with the Horwoods? Can't quite see our beloved MP buying a secondhand car from Pete McKerrin."

"I'm with you on that," Neal said. "For me, it sounds like there's a third party involved. The kidnappers got the money last night, and my guess is that it'd be with Pete – I'd reckon him for the brains of the duo from what I've heard of Doug. Perhaps he hasn't passed it on yet."

"We'd better get on to it quickly," Winter replied.

"There may be a way we can do that," Neal suggested, immediately claiming both his colleagues' full attention. He told them about the two men who'd recently offered Mal Brady a secondhand car. "We know the identity of one," Neal went on. "And it would tie in very nicely if the other was Pete McKerrin. Tom said he thought Pete might be up to no good, although he seems to have kept his hands clean up till now. How about we get Brady to see if he recognizes him?"

"And at the same time keep Pete under surveillance in case he passes the money on." Winter was on the same wavelength. "It's worth a shot, Neal."

They decided to send Sally along with Brady to Pete McKerrin's car lot. Mal would wait across the road to observe, while Sally would act as a potential customer, looking for a cheap, reliable runabout. "Get into his office, if you can, Dakers," Winter suggested. "Just in case Mr Horwood's suitcase happens to be lying around."

Sally agreed to go, although Neal could tell she was somewhat underwhelmed by the idea.

He was right. Firstly, she'd been ribbed about lurking in the bushes with DI Winter. Now she was on course for another ribbing by posing as DC Brady's girlfriend.

The joys of being a WDC.

21

If Pete McKerrin turned out to be one of the kidnappers, Sally would need to make sure she wasn't recognized, although the incident at the rendezvous the previous evening had taken place in total darkness, and her assailant hadn't had a look at her face.

However, it was agreed that she should go back to her digs to change, and that Brady would pick her up from there in an unmarked car. "And leave that ruddy mac in the boot, Mal," Neal implored him.

Sally changed into the smart two-piece suit and heels which she'd worn to Neal's wedding, let down her hair and applied some lipstick and rouge: someone's secretary on her way home from the office.

Mal Brady was waiting at the kerb and perked up noticeably as she got in beside him.

"Blimey, Dakers! On your way to Elstree for an audition?"

"It's Sally for this afternoon. And, incredibly, I'm supposed to be your bird. No, I can't believe it either."

"*Ooohh.* Then call me Mal, sugar, and let's meet up for a drink after work."

"Huh, some hopes. And you might at least have smartened up a bit."

"This is a new jacket," Mal protested.

"Right. Which jumble sale did you pick it up from?"

Disgruntled, Mal drove off. On reaching Cowley, they agreed he'd drop her round the corner from McKerrin's car lot and park across the road so that he'd have a good view of the man when he appeared.

Sally wobbled along the street – with her height she didn't usually go for heels – turned into the lot and started looking over the cars with a suitably unpracticed eye.

Pete McKerrin was quickly out of his little wooden shed of an office. It had to be him, bulky in a loud blue suit, dark, swept-back hair and amazingly white teeth bared in a predatory smile.

"Hello, darling. What can I do you for, then?"

Biting back a waspish retort, Sally smiled dizzily and explained that she was looking for a runabout to get her to and from the office.

"Have a dekko along at the end there. That Ford Popular, the little Simca, the green Standard Eight – all of 'em well under two hundred nicker. Never know your luck, I might be able to squeeze out an extra bit of discount, just for you."

Sally hoped he wasn't about to give her a conducted tour of each vehicle. She detested his closeness, the cloying aftershave which he must have bathed in. But she needn't have worried because after a few minutes his attention was seriously diverted when a gleaming white Sprite pulled into the lot and scrunched to a halt directly outside his office.

A woman squeezed out, bundled in a fur coat topped by a cascade of auburn hair. She switched McKerrin an imperious glance. "Hi, Pete, honey," she trilled. "How's tricks?" With a dismissive look at Sally, she sashayed decoratively in tight skirt and impossible heels towards the office door.

McKerrin practically sprinted after her like a faithful terrier. "All the better for seeing you, sweetheart."

With that last utterance, Sally realized Pete McKerrin had been her assailant at the rendezvous. Not too smitten to forget that he had a potential customer, he called back, "Have a butcher's and see what you fancy, love. Back in a jiffy."

Sally continued to inspect the line of cars, her full attention on the office door, which McKerrin had pulled shut behind him. *Got you – sweetheart,* she thought viciously. It would be an appropriate payback for the ordeal he'd put her through.

The woman was out within five minutes, and Sally got a good view of her. She put her in her early thirties, attractive, although her features were too sharp to be really pretty and made up to the hilt. Everything about her spoke money: someone's money, and Sally doubted it was McKerrin's.

And talking of money, a large brown envelope protruded from the top of her handbag, causing Sally to wonder if they might just have made a lucky strike.

McKerrin was working overtime to get the woman to stay, something about closing up early and driving out of town to some cosy restaurant he knew. But Sally could see from her set expression that she'd got what she'd come for, and he was wasting his time.

"Got to dash, Pete, honey." Sally found the breathless simpering of the woman's voice unbearable. "Be in touch soon." She wriggled back behind the wheel, flashing a shapely leg as she dumped her handbag on the passenger seat.

"Don't leave it too long, sweetheart," Pete threw back hungrily. But she'd started up and was already reversing away with an insulting puff of mashed gravel dusting his pristine trousers. A casual, parting wave, and she was gone, with McKerrin gazing longingly after her, but not before Sally had committed the Sprite's registration number to memory.

It then dawned on Pete that he still had a customer, but she was already making her way towards him.

"I like the little Simca," she said with a smile. "But I'll have to see if I can borrow the money from my dad."

Pete's face split in a smarmy grin. "No problem, I'd say, darling. You just smile at him sweetly, like you are now. Then pop back, and I'll run you round the block in it, but I promise you it's in good nick."

Sally promised she'd be back, neglecting to mention that it'd be complete with squad car, siren and handcuffs, and walked down and across the road to where Mal was parked. She looked over her shoulder before getting into the car to make sure McKerrin was back in his office.

"Get a good look at him?" she asked.

"He's not the bloke who tried to sell me the car." Mal sounded a bit dejected. "What about you?"

"Oh, he's one of the kidnappers alright. I recognized his voice. And the woman came out with a large brown envelope she didn't have on her way in."

"I was watching her from across the road."

"I bet you were."

"Yep, a real smasher." Mal grinned lasciviously. "But not a patch on you, Sal. So, where to now?"

Sally sighed. "Let's get back to the nick," she said. *"Sugar."*

*

Phil Winter and Neal were well pleased with the outcome of their colleagues' afternoon. Winter recognized the Sprite's registration number as a London plate and busied himself with phoning a contact in the Met to get a trace on the owner. Sally and Mal were practically at the end of their shifts by then, while Neal concentrated on his paperwork for another hour before calling it a day.

He reached home to a warm welcome from Jill, who was clearly relieved that he'd not had a brush with danger similar to that of the previous day. She'd prepared steak and chips, one of his favourite meals, for tea, along with a glass of Double Diamond. After their meal, they sat on the settee watching television for a while, Jill snuggling up to him. He knew exactly what she was about to say.

"Neal, darling. Did you manage to get those details?"

He didn't need to ask what details. Anne Barcham had been on Jill's mind since the previous morning, and he knew she'd been to visit her that afternoon.

"First of all, did you learn anything new?" he asked.

"She took me into her room at Silver Birches," Jill said. "It was so neat and tidy. The warden said that Anne's always offering to help out with chores around the home and seems very happy there when she keeps busy. Otherwise, her daughter's on her mind all the time, and Anne can get quite depressed. She keeps Jeanie's framed photograph in the centre of her mantelpiece, and all the time we were chatting and drinking tea, she never took her eyes off it. I felt so sorry for her."

"Did she tell you anything about her background?"

"She was a nurse during the war. That was how she met her husband, Joe. He was wounded overseas and brought back to England, where he ended up as one of Anne's patients. They married at the end of the war, by which time she was already pregnant with Jeanie. They moved to Oxford to live with Anne's mum.

"Joe spent long hours working, ensuring they had enough money to get by on, and he was never unkind to her. Anne never questioned what he did for a living – he was out a lot at night, and told her he worked in several pubs. His wage wasn't great, and she still needed to work for them to be comfortable.

"It was on one of the days when she was working that Joe decided to take Jeanie to the seaside for a few days. They never returned. That's all I've got, Neal. Did you find anything in Records?"

"Tom was able to point me in the way of more information. Joe Barcham had some form. He'd been inside before the war on a charge of breaking and entering. When he came out, he went into the army and saw service in North Africa and Italy. He was wounded during the D-Day invasion and invalided back to hospital in London, where he met Anne.

"As far as we can tell, Joe had a number of jobs, mainly bar work in local pubs, his last one being at the Rambling Rose down near the Plain. It's no longer there, but what is of interest is that it was owned by Willie Devlin. Devlin was suspected of all sorts of mischief, but there was never enough proof to convict him. It was reckoned that he had friends in high places, that he had something on them, and in return for his silence they bailed him out of any potential trouble. The last the manager of the Rambling Rose saw of Joe Barcham was when he left work one Friday night in an upbeat mood and looking forward to a holiday with his young daughter – her first holiday at the seaside – in Weymouth, he told his boss.

"Almost a week later, Joe's body was washed up along the Dorset coast. A couple of witnesses recalled someone of his description getting into a boat with two other men, but no-one could remember the little girl. If there was a boating accident, Joe's was the only body found. There was no sign of Jeanie or anyone else. Anne Barcham and her mother employed a private detective to look for Jeanie, but he drew a blank."

Jill had listened with a serious expression. Neal couldn't tell what she'd been hoping for, because the case was more than fifteen years old, and there were no further details to be had.

"Poor Anne," Jill said. "She firmly believes Jeanie's still alive. She'd be a bit younger than me – nineteen or twenty by now. "Oh, Neal, darling, please can you look into it? You see, I think she might be right. From what you say, Joe Barcham could well have been murdered. And if he was, would his killers have been heartless enough to have done away with a four-year-old girl? And you say the witnesses didn't remember seeing her? Might Joe have left her in someone's care?"

"Or might she just have drowned with Joe, and her body never recovered?" Neal suggested. "I'm sorry if that sounds harsh, darling, but it's the coldest of cold cases, and we're a small team working flat out at present on a couple of difficult investigations."

Jill took hold of his arm, a plea in her eyes. She was a naturally kind and compassionate girl, and he could tell that she felt the older woman's pain, the looming hopelessness of her dilemma.

"Oh, Neal, if there was just *something* we could do to set the poor woman's mind at rest. This has dragged on for fifteen years of her life. She's by no means an old woman – she could still move on. Every single person has their story, and hers deserves to be happier."

He took her in his arms. She meant so much to him, and he couldn't bear for her to be unhappy.

"Once things have settled down a bit, okay? I can't promise anything, but I might put Sally Dakers on to it."

Jill's expression cleared. "Sally would be first class. She's so sympathetic and would really relate to Anne. Oh, Neal, thank you."

"But not just yet, Jill, alright? The cases we're working on at the moment have to take priority, and I believe we may be getting somewhere with them both."

22

Neal was right in that progress wasn't far away. He was busy in his office the next morning when Mal Brady knocked and put his head round the door.

"Uncle Tom's got someone at the desk asking to see you, Gally. None other than our friend Mr Sanderson. I reckon he's come to confess."

"Don't be too confident about that, Mal. Although he has got a few more questions to answer. Wheel him along to the interview room, and we'll see him there."

Neal waited outside his office door for Brady to bring Sanderson along. The young man looked presentable in his light-grey suit, but his features were pinched and troubled. Neal wondered if Mal was about to be proved right. There was an aura of despondency about him - perhaps of guilt?

He greeted Sanderson and led the way to the interview room, showing him to a seat, while he and Mal took their places across the table from him.

"You wanted to see us, Mr Sanderson," Neal began pleasantly. "Have you got anything to add to what you told us the other day?"

"Yes, Sergeant." Bob cleared his throat noisily and fidgeted in his seat, a bentwood chair which wasn't the most comfortable. "This is going to sound strange, but I swear to you I'm not making it up. You see, I have a spare set of keys to my car, which I keep in my desk at the sales office. The other day, I couldn't find them and wondered if I might have taken them back to my digs by mistake. But I couldn't turn them up anywhere.

"First thing this morning, I had to call into the office to pick up some paperwork for today's appointments, and the keys were there in my drawer, underneath some documents."

"There's no way you might have missed seeing them before?"

Bob shook his head. "None at all. I'd taken out the contents of every drawer, and the keys were nowhere to be found."

"So, what you're saying is that someone from your company must have taken them?"

"I'm saying it's possible. And the keys went missing before my car was stolen."

"Then if someone took them, they'd have had access to your car. And when the Witney police found it, it hadn't been forcibly broken into. Therefore, keys were used to open and start it up, and that seems to point the finger at one of your colleagues."

"Yes. I – I suppose it does."

Brady had been studying Sanderson suspiciously, and it had added to the young man's discomfort. "Is this the truth, then, Mr Sanderson?" he asked. "It's not just you trying to get yourself off the hook and shift the blame on to someone you don't like?"

"And there wasn't a mention of the missing keys when you came to see us earlier in the week," Neal threw in reasonably. "You knew you had a spare set of keys. Hadn't you thought to look in your desk when the car went missing?" He fixed the young man with a stern stare. "I'm afraid this doesn't look good, sir. We spoke to Witney police yesterday as a matter of routine. They seemed surprised that there was no real damage to your car. No marks on the door, supposing the thief had levered it open, and the wiring hadn't been disturbed. It makes sense that someone must have used a key."

Bob Sanderson looked hunted. "The keys had been missing for a few days," he said. "I'm sorry, Sergeant Gallian. You see, I was worried about Avril and simply wasn't thinking straight. The car was found quickly, and I was so glad to get it back that I honestly didn't give the matter another thought, guessed that I must have mislaid them somewhere. I – I know it all sounds very thin, but I promise that I'm telling the truth…"

Mal was obviously sceptical and didn't bother to hide it. Neither was Neal convinced, although he believed they could badger the young man until they were blue in the face and get no further. It was something they could come back to if necessary, but for the time being he decided he'd give Sanderson the benefit of the doubt, even though he knew Mal wouldn't be with him on that.

"Okay, Mr Sanderson," he said. "Let's follow this up and see where it goes." He ignored Mal's questioning glance. "So, is there anyone with access to the sales office who might have a grudge against you?"

Bob was fidgeting furiously, a line of perspiration on his forehead. The words seemed to jerk out reluctantly. "Well, yes, there's one. His name's Tony Swires. He – he's a fellow rep."

"What's his problem with you?"

"He's always been good at his job. Up to just over two years ago, he represented the South Midlands area. There was some -er, trouble with a female buyer. He could have lost his job, but the sales manager, Mike Braddon, gave him another chance. Swires moved to the South-West region and has done well there. Jack Lumsden took over South Midlands, but when the London rep retired a year or so later, Jack, as senior sales rep, got the London patch.

"Tony Swires had worked hard to repay Mike Braddon's faith in him, and he might have expected to get South Midlands back. But Mike offered it to a colleague, my friend Gordon Childers. Gordon's our rep for Wales and the North-West, and he'd recently taken out a mortgage on a cottage in the Welsh Marches. He turned the job down and recommended me. I'm the sales force's most junior member, and when Mike offered me the job and I accepted it, Swires took it badly. He's had a down on me ever since, and my worry is that if he got to know about my -er, friendship with Avril, he might use it against me."

"You've never mentioned to anyone about Mrs Walden?"

"Only to Gordon, who's a good friend. And he certainly wouldn't say anything to Swires – the pair of them don't get on."

"So, you're fairly certain Mr Swires doesn't know about your friendship with Mrs Walden?"

"I don't think he can. I'm sure he would have alluded to it before now or even told Mike Braddon in an attempt to drop me in it."

Neal nodded. "Right, Mr Sanderson. We'll need to take this further and arrange interviews with Mr Swires and Mr Braddon."

"Er, Mike's away this week at a conference in the North-East, and Tony's on the road in Devon. But Mike'll be back in the office on Monday, and all the reps will be there for a sales meeting on Wednesday."

"It'd make sense to see them then. I'll contact Mr Braddon on Monday and set it up. Mr Sanderson, I must ask you to say nothing about this to anyone. Anyone at all, is that clear?"

"You have my word, Sergeant," Bob replied solemnly. He pushed back his chair and stood up. He looked pensive. "Sergeant Gallian, you probably think I'm being a sneak. I don't like Tony Swires, but I assure you I'm not trying to accuse him. It's just that, well, I realize I'm under suspicion. I swear I'm innocent, and I want to clear my name."

Neal felt the young man was being straight with them. As he listened to what Bob was saying, he couldn't help thinking of Dennis Nolan. Something the two of them had in common was that they were earnest young men trying to forge an honest path through a disbelieving world. And he was determined to give Bob Sanderson a chance.

He could tell that Mal wasn't convinced, so he thanked Bob and accompanied him to the station's front door himself, rather than entrust him to his colleague's tender care.

On his return, Mal had sidled out of the interview room, and Neal pointed him towards his office. "Not won you over, has he?" he said.

Mal frowned. "Meaning you believe him? Come off it, Gally, you surely can't believe that lame excuse about the car keys?"

"He's not off the hook, Mal, and he's in danger of painting himself into a corner. But if he's guilty, why would he come up with such a naïve excuse as a stolen set of keys? It's paper-thin. And yes, for the moment I'd give him the benefit of the doubt and look in Tony Swires' direction. Remember, Oxford was on his sales patch for a while. There's a possibility he may have crossed paths with Jerry Rudd."

Mal took this on board, nodding thoughtfully. "You're ahead of me, Gally. Yes, there could be something in it."

"I'll contact Cheltenham CID and get the nod from them for us to pay a visit to X-Pressive. Then on Monday I'll phone Mike Braddon and give him some pretext for us coming there next Wednesday, because I don't want Swires warned off. As for you, Mal, once you've fortified yourself in the canteen, I'd like you to check the records for Tony Swires, then if that draws a blank, phone Cheltenham to see if they've got anything on him."

Mal went on his way, and Neal dropped by to update Phil Winter on what had just happened and what he intended to set in motion the following week.

Winter had been about to call Neal in anyway. The Met had got back to him quickly with a trace on the Sprite. It was registered to a Karina Dorn at an address in Finchley. According to information received, Miss Dorn was a nightclub hostess, occupying a smart apartment in a quiet mews. *Somebody's money,* as Sally had guessed.

"I've asked a colleague to stake out the flat," Winter went on, "and I'm on my way up there this afternoon to oversee operations. I've put in a request for photographs to be taken of each visitor over the weekend and into next week to see if we can find any connection with Horwood. My money's on some political enemy. I dare say he's made a few."

Neal was glad to see Phil Winter's enthusiasm coming to the fore. Despite one or two setbacks that week, he reckoned the man was a decent detective. It had, after all, been a difficult week for him, and Neal knew the DCI hadn't given Winter an easy time of it. Oxford had been Pilling's patch for a long time, and while Neal could understand his Guv'nor's frustration at being temporarily sidelined, he could also feel sympathy for Winter.

"You've plenty to be getting on with here, haven't you, Neal?" Winter asked before leaving for London.

Neal replied in the affirmative, although he felt it a pity that his main concern couldn't be followed up until after the weekend. A little while later, Mal Brady reported back that neither Oxford nor Cheltenham had anything on file concerning Tony Swires. Did Neal want him to check further afield? But Neal decided to draw the line there. He hadn't really expected Mal to find anything and didn't feel disappointed.

Because he had a feeling about Tony Swires…

23

Jill knew Neal had had a busy week: not only had there been the murder investigation and bank incident but a lot of minor issues to resolve and reports to write. She'd hoped she could help him enjoy a relaxing weekend, but by the middle of Saturday morning, she felt like kicking herself.

She'd had her eye on a Bex Bissell carpet cleaner for the flat. Neal had agreed to buy it and said they'd drive into town and pick it up at the weekend.

She'd always used Mr Hobbs' hardware shop in Cowley Road when she'd kept house for her Uncle Lam at Braxbury and knew he priced his goods competitively, so they parked in a side street and went along to the shop to make the purchase.

Mr Hobbs, a round, cheerful man of fifty in a spotless brown overall, assiduously wrote out a receipt. "Now, let's see. It's Miss Westmacott, isn't it?"

"Oh no," Jill replied, with a fond glance at her husband. "I'm married now. It's Mrs Gallian."

"Gallian?" Mr Hobbs was staring at Neal and looking stunned. "Then – my goodness, you must have been that young policeman who…?"

Neal was ahead of his wife and putting on a brave face. "That's right, Mr Hobbs. We never met, did we, circumstances being what they were? I heard you didn't come out of it too well either?"

It had just dawned on Jill what they were talking about, and how she should have realized what the consequences might be in calling into Mr Hobbs' shop. And how it was too late to change matters now.

Because Hobbs was in full flow. "Well, I never expected it, you see, Mr Gallian. It was early evening, and I should have locked up by then, but I was working on some stock figures, and I suppose I'd left the door open because you always hope that big, late sale will walk in. Served me right, really, and cured me forever of that particular notion. It was a cold night, and he had a scarf round his face, so I wasn't suspicious at all. He mumbled some question about – what was it now? – a coal scuttle, I think. I took him to the back of the shop to show him what we had, and when I turned round, lo and behold, there he was with a gun in his hand and ordering me to empty the till. Well, I was never so scared in all my life. My heart was a-thumping, and I didn't think my legs'd bear me up as far as the till. But when he prodded me in the back with that there gun, I made it alright, opened the till and stuffed the notes in a bag. All of a sudden, he was gone, the door slammed, and I snatched up the phone and dialled 999. Whew! I shall never forget it till my dying day. And you, sir? Are you fully recovered?

Jill could tell that Neal had to work on a smile. "Yes, Mr Hobbs. And now happily married into the bargain."

"I'm very glad to hear it, sir. And miss – or should I say madam? Many congratulations to you both. But - did they ever catch him?"

"No, I'm afraid he slipped through our fingers."

"I'm sorry to hear it."

Mr Hobbs busied himself with the receipt, they shook hands, wished each other good day, and Jill and Neal set off with their purchase.

Jill was horribly embarrassed, apologizing to her husband the moment they were outside the shop.

"Oh, Neal, I'm so sorry. I should have known…"

His tone was placatory. "There was no way you could have known, darling. I'd never met Mr Hobbs before today, because DCI Pilling took over the investigation immediately after it happened."

He was doing a good job covering up his feelings, but Jill knew that inside, in that private place, he'd be reliving the horrors of that day, memories of Clyde in life as well as in death. For months now, he'd succeeded in keeping his demons at bay, in fact since Terry Arden's death; Arden, murdered by the man Neal called the Face. He'd almost been mown down himself as the Face's car had roared away from the scene.

Jill had wondered how long that old obsession might linger, how it would affect him that the man had eluded his grasp again. But Don Pilling had immediately taken him off the case, sternly warned him to concentrate on the numerous other matters which formed their caseload.

And Neal had knuckled down, applied himself to his work, got himself made up to Detective Sergeant, with help and support from the DCI, Tom Wrightson and Sally Dakers. Jill herself, too: always mindful of steering him clear of the haunting past, the poisonous memories.

But she knew he couldn't entirely forget, wondered if he ever would.

She tried her best, though. After lunch at the flat, they went for a long walk on Shotover, and she cooked him a tasty shepherd's pie for tea, washed down with a bottle of brown ale.

The next day, Sunday, Lambert Wilkie had invited them out to Braxbury, where he and Neal were to take part in a clay pigeon shoot at a farm down the lane from Wilkie's house, Briar Hedge. Jill and the other ladies had agreed to provide and serve refreshments.

It proved a tonic for him – for her too, after Saturday's *faux pas*, and as the men came into the barn for the buffet their womenfolk had prepared, she was glad to see him chatting companionably away with her uncle and several others, his immediate reaction being to walk over and greet her with a kiss.

Afterwards, Jill and Neal walked back through the woods to Briar Hedge, where they had a cup of tea with Wilkie, put matters to rights in his untidy kitchen and made their way back to Headington.

Jill was happy that Neal was back to his normal self, but she was mindful that only a battle had been won, not the war.

*

Monday morning, however, proved a further tonic in more ways than one. Tom Wrightson looked up from the desk as Neal walked into the station. "Man in charge wants to see you, lad," he greeted him bluntly. "As in right away."

Neal thanked him and went down the corridor, wondering if Winter might have hit a brick wall in his London operation. He knocked on the door and opened it to walk into a cloud of smoke, recognizing a familiar face through the haze.

"Guv!"

He looked back along the corridor at Tom, whose weatherbeaten face bore a broad smile and gave him a thumbs-up.

"In you come, DS Gallian."

Pilling had risen to his feet with some difficulty, and the two men shook hands.

"Welcome back, Guv."

"It's good to be back, Neal," came the brisk reply. "Sitting around home is not for me." He chuckled sardonically. "Sheila's not too keen on it, either." He caught a movement in the corridor: Yvonne Begley on her way past. "Oh, WPC Begley? Could you organize some tea for us, please?"

Yvonne looked in, beaming. "A pleasure, Mr Pilling."

Over their tea and digestives, Neal updated his boss on where they'd got to so far.

"Yes," Pilling replied, "Tom said DI Winter had taken himself back off to London. Once he's back here and cleared his – my – desk, he can return full-time to the Met with my blessing. I shall recommend that his secondment is made permanent. I'm sure I can persuade the ACC to back me up." Neal noticed a small pile of papers on top of the filing cabinet, while the DCI's previously abandoned documents were now back in their customary place, strewn across his desk. Winter wouldn't need to do much clearing.

Pilling went on to say that he'd phone Cheltenham CID on Neal's behalf, as he was on good terms with his counterpart there. He'd get him to arrange a meeting with Mike Braddon and his sales team for Wednesday morning, when Neal would be present. Nothing would be said to Braddon regarding the Oxford angle.

"And what the heck have you done with Brady?" was the DCI's parting shot. "Tom reckons he's in line for a commendation. You too, by the way."

"Brady did it all by himself, Guv," Neal said. "There are still the rough edges, but he's worked hard on this case, and I've not had to push him. There's a good DC in there somewhere, and a loyal colleague. He saved my life last week, and there's no way I shall forget that."

"Well, miracles *do* happen," Pilling exclaimed. "That's got to be good for him and for us. Let's make sure the progress continues."

He wasn't wrong. Indeed, Mal Brady seemed to be on something of a roll. Later that morning, a knock on Neal's door was succeeded by the entrance of a flushed and grinning Brady.

"I've seen him, Gally."

Neal glanced up from what he was doing. "Seen who, Mal?"

"Him. The second bloke of the pair who tried to sell me the car. Just now, round in Market Street."

Neal frowned. "Why didn't you follow him, then? See where he went?"

Mal's grin stretched wider. "No need. He was busy hoisting somebody's car up onto his breakdown truck, and there was his name and telephone number on the truck's door. I've just looked him up in the directory: Stan Timmins, with a workshop off North Hinksey Lane."

Neal returned the grin. "No stopping you, is there, DC Brady? Good work. Let's get round there and take a couple of uniforms as back-up. I'm banking on your Mr Timmins being half of one dodgy operation."

*

The doors of Stan Timmins' workshop stood open, the breakdown truck parked outside. He had a car up on a ramp, and as Neal and Mal walked in, they heard the clunk of a spanner and spotted a man in oily overalls busy beneath the car.

Mal strolled past him and began inspecting various car parts stored on dexion shelving to the side of the workshop. A Morris Minor, parked towards the rear, looked as if it had been recently resprayed.

The spanner suddenly clattered to the floor, and the man loomed out from beneath the car. He was large, jowly and forty-something, with a thatch of greasy dark hair and a face which looked as if it didn't find smiling easy.

"Oi! Who the heck are you? And what d'you mean by coming and poncing around in here?"

Neal showed his warrant card. "Oxford CID, Mr Timmins."

"You can't just walk in here like this." There was suddenly less aggression, and the man spoke in an injured tone. But he flared up again, as his gaze moved round to where Mal stood beside the shelving. "And what do you think you're up to?" he asked accusingly.

"Just admiring your little collection of number plates," Mal replied easily.

"Well, admire 'em and come away from there," Timmins growled. "This is a legitimate business, I'll have you know. Anyway, you want to look the place over, you'd better get a search warrant."

Ignoring the remark, Neal nodded towards the Morris Minor. "Looks a nice little runabout."

"Yes, it is. What about it? You interested or summat?"

"Certainly interested in running a trace on its number plate. Don't think I'll need a warrant for that."

Neal was close enough to Timmins to catch the glint of apprehension in his eyes. But the man tried to bluster it out.

"You go ahead, then, pal. Me and my mate worked hard on that car, bought it legit and done it up legit. You go on back to your nick and check it out, and then we'll see who's right."

Mal Brady had been standing to the side enjoying the conversation. Now he stepped forward, the movement claiming Timmins' attention.

"Perhaps we'll do that," he said. "And then when we get back here, we'll find you've done a runner."

"Fair point," Neal agreed. "Why don't you come back with us, Mr Timmins, and enjoy a sit-down and a cup of tea while we look into it? Nothing for you to worry about anyway, is there, since it's all legit?"

"Oh, Gawd." Stan Timmins' face went white behind its oily sheen, and his bravado left him as quickly as air from a punctured beach ball. He pulled forward a stool, sank down onto it and sighed. "I knew it couldn't last." He looked up helplessly at Neal. "Sure, the car's dodgy," he went on, "but, true as I sit here, this wasn't my idea."

"But these are your premises."

"Yeah, but it's down to this mate of mine, see? He had this idea, and I let him use the workshop, 'cause he lent me money to tide me through when business was bad. I just wasn't in a position to say no. Honest, I – I can explain it all…"

"You're about to get the chance," Mal said, as a squad car drew up, and Paul Hodgson and a colleague got out and approached the workshop. "If you'd accompany these officers, Mr Timmins, DC Brady and I will be with you shortly."

"I'd like to change out of these overalls first."

"Fine. We'll wait with you while you do."

"And – and I'll give you my mate's address."

"Thanks, but we already know it."

Once Timmins had changed, locked up and, emptied of all aggression, been taken back to the station in the squad car, Neal and Mal drove the short distance to Faversham Close in Botley. Mal beat gleefully on the door of Number 53, for it to be finally and violently wrenched open by an angry man in striped pyjamas.

"Look, what is it? I got a long night shift tonight, and I need some kip." He gasped and took a step back, as he recognized the callers.

"You can catch up on your sleep at our place, Mr Walden," Neal advised him. "Once you've answered a few questions, that is. We'll come in and wait while you get dressed."

"And just so's you know," Mal added with a wicked grin, "your mate Stan's dropped you right in it."

In fact, probably the same distance Neville Walden's jaw dropped, as the two detectives entered the house and ushered him back upstairs.

"Our Neville wasn't averse to nicking a few parts from the works," Mal said, a couple of hours later, when both men had been interviewed. They'd tried to blame 'this bloke we met in a pub – he wasn't local – he sort of got us into it. And he was the type you wouldn't say no to'; and then each other and were currently locked in adjacent cells feeling sorry for themselves, and no longer the best of friends. "As well as doing up and selling stolen cars which got passed on to them, CID up in Brum'll appreciate getting hold of a couple of the names of those contacts they've just given us."

Neal smiled and nodded along to Mal's comments. He was thinking of Avril Walden's reaction when he'd gone round to Paper, Pen & Ink to break to her the news of her husband's arrest.

She'd been far from devastated. And when her husband came out of clink in a couple of years' time, Neal didn't think it likely that Avril would be waiting for him.

24

Phil Winter phoned Neal at the station early on Tuesday morning. Neal gathered that Winter and Don Pilling had had a discussion the previous day. The DCI, though not yet fully fit, was back in charge with ACC Streatley's blessing, and Winter would return to the Met. Neal imagined that, in the face of the DCI's determination, his superior had capitulated fairly easily.

Not that Winter seemed at all put out, sounding very enthusiastic. "Things are about to move up a gear, Neal," he said. "We're planning to raid Karina Dorn's apartment later today. Saturday night's the only time she's been out, when she went to work at the Twilight Club. Given the outfit she was wearing, there was no way she might have had the money on her, and I had a couple of officers watching her all the time. I'll give you the okay when to pick up the McKerrin brothers."

The DCI had requested that an officer from Oxford should travel up to London to see the operation through with Winter, and Neal had suggested Sally Dakers, who'd been involved with it from the beginning. Winter had had no problem with that. "Tell her she'll be in for a big surprise," was his enigmatic parting comment.

Neal called Sally in and informed her that she'd be taking the next train up to London, where she'd liaise with DI Winter at the police station in Finchley. He mentioned Winter's promise of a 'big surprise', and when she told Yvonne and Pam about it before leaving, they ribbed her good-naturedly. "If he offers to take you up to an attic to show you his etchings, you know you're in trouble," Pam warned her. "Still, doubt if you'd want to see 'em anyway."

But Sally was simply glad to be included in what was a predominantly male set-up and to be there at the conclusion of the case.

*

As far as Sally was concerned, the 'big surprise' was Winter himself. He greeted her warmly and introduced her to one of the officers who was on his London team, WDC Gethin. "Dakers will be with us as an observer," he said. "She's worked hard on this case, and it's only right that she should be in at the death." Praise, indeed!

He took her along to the office he was using. "Come and have a look through the mugshots of the lovely Miss Dorn's visitors over the weekend," he invited her. "Gethin here is a very competent photographer, and I'm sure there'll be a face you'll recognize."

Sally was truly taken aback when she saw it: the face of someone she'd never have suspected.

She went along with Winter and his team to witness the arrest of Karina Dorn, who greeted them with a torrent of distinctly unladylike phrases. Winter's production of a warrant silenced her, and half-a-dozen officers piled into her apartment to conduct a search. The money was quickly found: four thousand pounds in used notes, so they presumed the McKerrin brothers would have the rest.

Karina Dorn had begun by colourfully denying everything. According to her, the money had been a gift from a rich patron of the Twilight Club. But once Winter mentioned that detectives from Oxford CID had witnessed her visit to McKerrin's car lot on the previous Thursday afternoon and had seen her coming out with the bulging envelope which they'd just found behind her bookshelves, she folded. She explained that she'd met McKerrin at the club a few weeks earlier, and they'd become friendly. He'd duped her into providing him with information about the Horwood family, threatening violence if she didn't comply. No matter that she'd 'felt so helpless with no-one to turn to', her 'little girl lost in the big, bad city' act made no impression on Winter, and she was arrested and taken in for questioning.

*

As soon as Neal received Phil Winter's call that they'd apprehended Karina Dorn, he put together a team to tackle the McKerrins.

They called in first at the car lot where Pete, at his most unctuous, was in the middle of a sales pitch to a couple who quickly excused themselves and hurried away at the sight of a squad car bearing four police officers drawing in.

"You might have a wander round some of these cars, Mal, and make a note of their registration numbers," Neal suggested to Brady. "Strikes me Pete mightn't have been averse to colluding with Messrs Walden and Timmins and their various contacts."

"I'll get on to it, Gally," Mal replied. "Could be another link in a very long chain."

They escorted Pete along to his office. He'd been spotted with Karina Dorn the other day, so couldn't pretend he didn't know her. Winter had suggested Neal might try McKerrin with Dorn's excuse that he'd manipulated her into it. Neal did, and it resulted in fireworks.

"I never did, I swear it! It was her idea all along, the cow! And she was getting the lion's share of the dosh, not us who'd done all the hard graft!" The rest of Pete's tirade was unprintable.

Once he was safely under lock and key, they drove out to Hillberry Farm to bring in his brother. Doug McKerrin proved to be more troublesome and, anticipating he might not be the type to come quietly, Neal left Hodgson and Palgrave in the car outside the farm entrance, while he and Brady went in on foot.

Doug saw them before they spotted him and began hurrying away towards a barn. The detectives broke into a run but were still some way off when they heard the revving of a motorbike. Head down over the handlebars, McKerrin tore out of the barn, forcing Neal and Mal to leap out of his path.

He hadn't reckoned on the squad car. The moment they heard the bike, Paul Hodgson drove up to the farm entrance. For a moment, it seemed there'd be a collision, but Doug, in a mad bid to escape, saw a gap between the car and the gatepost and went for it.

He was hampered by the sidecar. As he squeezed the machine through the opening, the sidecar's wheel clipped the post, tipping the bike off balance. Doug tried to right it but ended up slewing across the narrow road, the bike ending in the hedge and its rider in the ditch.

A semi-conscious McKerrin brother was taken back to Oxford, where a doctor checked him out and confirmed that he was fit enough to be questioned before long.

*

Early that evening, Phil Winter, accompanied by Sally Dakers, called at a small flat in a three-storey building in the corner of a square in Pimlico. The door was opened after a minute or so, but only after a volley of disgruntled huffing and puffing from behind it.

"Ah, Winter. It's you." Dalton Horwood, in shirtsleeves and no tie, still succeeded in being at his most high-handed. He clutched a sheaf of papers at his side. "I'm afraid I've no time for this now, as I'm due at the House shortly. As I'm sure I'd informed you, this is a busy week. But I take it you'll have recovered my money?"

"We've made an arrest, sir. And I've just now received the intelligence that two more have been made in Oxford. Er, forgive me, Mr Horwood, but I believe it'd be best if we came in."

The MP looked affronted. "I don't know if you heard me, Winter, but as I said, I'm in a hurry. We can talk here, if we must, but you'll need to be quick about it."

"As you wish, sir." Winter was at his formal best, his face wearing an appropriately constipated expression. "Mr Horwood, I believe you're acquainted with a Miss Karina Dorn?"

Sally registered the flash of alarm in the MP's eyes. "Karina Dorn? Er, I can't say that I know the name."

On cue, Sally brandished the photographs with which she'd been entrusted and held them out in front of Horwood.

"Perhaps you'd like to think again, sir." Winter's voice held a proper note of sternness. "These photographs were taken by one of my colleagues last evening. As you'll see, the one on the left shows you entering Miss Dorn's apartment at 7.21pm, and the other clearly shows you coming out of there a little over two hours later."

"Um, er, perhaps you'd better step inside." The MP was already wilting, his voice little more than a croak. He sank on to a chair beside the hallstand, while Sally closed up the door behind them. "Er, Miss Dorn. Yes, of course – forgive me, Inspector, I must have misheard the name. Miss Dorn carries out a – er, um, ah, a little secretarial work on my behalf."

"We've not long relieved her of most of your money, Mr Horwood." Winter was relentless now, his manner imperious. "I believe my Oxford colleague, DS Gallian, is on the point of recovering the rest. Karina Dorn was friendly with an Oxford secondhand car dealer, Peter McKerrin. He and his brother have confessed to being your daughter's kidnappers, and I believe further questioning will reveal that Karina Dorn was the prime mover in Miss Horwood's abduction."

"Karina?" Horwood's world was in tatters, his face grey, and his words came out in a helpless flood. "But no, I – I simply can't believe it of her. Such a dear, sweet girl. The times I've confided in her, the things I've told her, and she was such a patient listener when I poured out my troubles. Oh, Inspector Winter, I beg you. I – I can't afford a scandal, the party can't, not so soon after Profumo. I'm sure if you and I – both staunch Cambridge men, what? – if we – we sat down with my solicitor, perhaps we might be able to…?"

But Phil Winter was in full control, quickly overriding Horwood's desperate plea. "I'll pretend I didn't hear that, sir. Karina Dorn engineered the kidnapping of your daughter. That's a plain, unassailable fact. If you recall, Miss Horwood was held prisoner for three days in most uncomfortable conditions. It's fortunate that her treatment wasn't any worse. I'm sure, sir, that you wouldn't want to gloss over this. The Metropolitan Police and Oxford CID certainly aren't prepared to do so."

Horwood held up a meek hand in surrender. "Of course, Inspector. Poor Cressida. Yes, yes, you're right. I can't turn a blind eye to that. I-I'll co-operate fully."

"Thank you, sir. We'll leave it there for now and be back in touch shortly. You'll, er, soon be needing to go to your debate."

Dalton Horwood was studying the floor, the portrait of a man totally deflated. He shook his head sadly. "This has all come as rather a shock. I mean, I didn't know, would never have guessed… *Karina?* I simply can't believe… What's that you say? The debate? Oh, I – I'm really not sure if I shall be going now…"

*

Sally was late back to Oxford that evening but decided to phone Neal when she reached her digs, and they swapped accounts of the afternoon and evening events. Before she left London, she'd had to maintain a diplomatic silence when Phil Winter had been congratulated by his Divisional Superintendent on a successful operation. Winter had glowed with self-satisfaction but at least he'd had the grace to mention that he'd been ably supported by his teams in Oxford and London. His career looked to be heading upwards, but Sally believed that Oxford wouldn't feature any longer in its trajectory.

    She and Neal agreed that the end result of the case would see Marjorie Horwood deservedly come into her own, and that her husband, if he remained in that elevated state, might in future treat her, Cressida and Dennis Nolan with a little more respect.

25

X-Pressive Stationery Supplies occupied a large warehouse just off the A40 on the north side of Cheltenham. Neal and Mal Brady were met there early on the Wednesday morning by Tim Maddox, a keen young detective sergeant from the local station.

Maddox took them inside and introduced them to Mike Braddon, X-P's sales manager, a florid, shirt-sleeved man who, though greeting them with a ready smile and meaty handshake, looked understandably mystified.

Don Pilling's Cheltenham counterpart had spoken to Braddon at length two days previously, but Tim Maddox summarized it for everyone's benefit. He explained that Cheltenham CID were co-operating with Oxford, who were following up a link to a murder in the city ten days earlier. They thought one of Braddon's reps might be able to help identify a car which had been parked near the scene and glimpsed around the county on other occasions.

Maddox's explanation was necessarily cryptic, and Mike Braddon admitted that he was confused.

"I really don't see how much help we can give you, gents," he said. "Only Bob Sanderson visits the Oxford area through his work, the others only socially, if at all, and they all live some distance away. I'll go along with this if you think it'll be useful, but I trust it doesn't mean you suspect one of my reps of being involved in murder?"

At a nod from Maddox, Neal took charge. "Thanks, Mr Braddon. I'm not at liberty to answer your question, but we appreciate your co-operation and apologize for any confusion. We'd like to have a word with Mr Swires first, if we may."

"Tony?" Braddon looked puzzled. "He's not here yet. In fact, I'm not expecting anyone for the next fifteen or twenty minutes. He's not involved with Oxford anymore, so surely there's -? He paused, met by Neal's uncompromising expression, and shrugged. "Come on, I'll put you in the meeting room and send them in one by one as they arrive."

Maddox shook hands and made himself scarce, inviting Neal to telephone him at the station if he needed him for anything else. Neal and

Mal settled themselves behind the long table in the meeting room and made small talk with Braddon until the reps started to filter in.

As luck would have it, Tony Swires was first to arrive. They heard Braddon telling him about the forthcoming interview and had no problem hearing Swires express his extreme displeasure. Braddon told him bluntly that the police needed to see him, that he couldn't give him a reason, and sent him into the meeting room.

He stormed through the doorway and came to an abrupt halt, aware that the two detectives were staring at him. For the briefest moment, as he first set eyes on the man, Neal experienced something like an electric charge of recognition. It was a dull day, and the light in the room wasn't good. But Neal couldn't help wondering if he might have met Tony Swires before. There was a definite similarity to the face he'd glimpsed at an Oxford warehouse window almost three years previously…

Swires was in his thirties, thin with wispy dark hair, an apology for a beard and restless eyes in a petulant face. His suit looked lived-in, and his tie dangled loosely from around his neck. He stalked into the room, emboldened by resentment, switching a suspicious glance from Brady to Neal, as the latter calmly invited him to sit and made the introductions. Collecting his thoughts, Neal put on hold the idea that he recognized Swires from that time before. But he knew that he couldn't dismiss it completely.

Tony Swires dragged out a chair and sat. "Mind telling me what all this is about?" he asked truculently.

"I'm just about to," Neal replied stiffly. "We're looking into the death of an Oxford man named Jerry Rudd. His name ring any bells with you?"

"None. Never heard of him."

"You've not been to Oxford recently?"

"No call to go there anymore."

"But you used to?"

Swires gave him a hard stare. "Well, yes, 'cause it was on my sales patch. But that was more than two years ago."

"It's Bob Sanderson's patch now. How do you get on with him?"

"Okay." Swires' sour expression suggested otherwise.

"Do you like him?"

The man shrugged carelessly, not wanting to be drawn. "Not a question of liking. He's a colleague. A bit inexperienced, but he's learning."

"Why did you move from the South Midlands sales patch, Mr Swires?"

Swires threw Neal an unfriendly glance and didn't reply immediately. When he did, he mumbled his reply grudgingly. "Some trouble."

"What sort of trouble?"

"Look, is this necessary? There's Braddon out there being all mysterious, and you not telling me what all these ruddy questions are in aid of. I can tell you're after me for something. What the hell am I supposed to have done?"

"Nothing as far as we know, Mr Swires." Neal was the epitome of calm, his bland expression giving nothing away. "But I'll ask again. What sort of trouble?"

Tony Swires flung himself back in his chair and directed an exasperated epithet at the ceiling. "I got over-friendly with a female buyer," he grunted at last. "Although *she* gave *me* the come-on. Her husband complained to Braddon, and I got moved to another area."

"And this was in Oxford?"

"Yes, damn you, in Oxford."

Neal wondered if Paper, Pen & Ink might have been the store in question, although he couldn't envisage a woman like Avril Walden getting involved with Tony Swires. When he asked the question, Swires gave the name of a different store in another part of the city.

"And when the South Midlands area was freed up earlier in the year, did you apply?"

"The buyer who'd given me trouble had moved on, and I told Braddon I might be interested. Apart from London, it's the area with the biggest sales. You'd expect him to give it to someone with the necessary experience, wouldn't you?"

"And he didn't?"

"Well, he didn't give it to me. Acknowledged that I'd worked hard on my patch, but he thought I was better off where I was for the time being. No, he offered it to Gordon Childers as the next in line after me. Childers turned it down. He was happy with Wales and the North-West, and in any case was just about to buy a house in the area. Then the ruddy twerp recommended Sanderson, the two of them being good mates."

"You don't sound too happy about it?"

"Happy?" Swires spat out the word. "Too true I wasn't happy. Childers is a wet week of Sundays, and Braddon's daft enough to take his advice and hand the job to a novice like Sanderson." He paused, his lip curling in a nasty grin. "Still, from what I hear, our boy Robert's gaining *some* sort of experience. Be a pity if Mike Braddon ever got to hear about it…"

"Oh? What do you mean by that?"

"Well, it seems he's having a bit of fun on the side."

"He told you that, did he?"

Something in Neal's tone pulled Swires up sharply, making him realize that he might have said too much. He looked away, shrugged uncomfortably. "Office gossip," he muttered.

"So, who told you?"

Swires hesitated. Neal could almost hear his brain whirring, wondering whether he should give someone's name in the hope of deflecting suspicion from himself. Then he realized that all the reps would be present that day, and Neal was at liberty to question each of them.

He threw up his hands in surrender. "Alright, I saw a letter in his desk drawer."

"Why were you looking in there? With Mr Sanderson's permission?"

"He was out of the office. I was looking for a stapler and didn't think he'd mind. I just happened to see this letter from some woman friend. I mean, it was right there. I couldn't help but notice it. Stupid ruddy place to leave it, if you ask me."

Neal held the man's stare long enough for him to feel embarrassed and lower his gaze. He let an uncomfortable silence set in. Finally, he said, "You've obviously got an issue with Bob Sanderson."

Swires was immediately on the offensive. "What d'you mean, an issue? Look, Sergeant, how about you playing straight with me? Questions, questions and more ruddy questions. Okay, so I got a butcher's at some flippin' letter he might not have wanted me to see. So what? Is that a crime? Let me ask you again: *what am I supposed to have done?*"

Neal leaned forward, elbows on the table, while Mal Brady, looking grim, shifted noisily in his seat. For some reason, their movements seemed to further unsettle Swires, who looked apprehensively from one to the other and sat back in his chair.

"A company car was stolen," Neal said briskly. "And a spare set of keys was taken from one of your colleague's desk drawers. The car was seen parked near the spot where a man named Jerry Rudd was stabbed before being drowned in the Oxford canal."

"So, how does that tie in with me?" Swires was trying to recapture some of his former belligerence. "This is about Sanderson, isn't it? I keep my ear to the ground, see, and I heard about his car being stolen and then miraculously found undamaged the next day. Makes you wonder if he stole the blasted thing himself."

"I don't think he did, Mr Swires." Neal's voice was level, cold. "I believe it might have been taken by one of his colleagues, possibly someone who was in the habit of riffling through people's desk drawers. So, let me ask you the question I'm going to put to each of your fellow reps. Where were you on the night of Sunday 15th November – ten days ago – between 7pm and midnight?"

He'd expected Swires to hesitate, to need thinking time. But, to his surprise, the answer came back promptly. "In Weston-Super-Mare."

"Can anyone vouch for that?"

"Yes, I was with my son. My wife walked out two years ago and took him with her. I'm allowed to spend a weekend with him every fortnight – he was staying at my mum's. That's where I was, Sergeant. They'll both vouch for me." He reached into a pocket for a notebook and pen, scribbled something in it, tore out the page and slapped it down in front of Neal. "Mum's phone number. She'll tell you I was there all night, that I left at seven=thirty in the morning for an appointment in Taunton, and that I drove off in my own car, not ruddy Bob Sanderson's."

Neal handed Brady the slip of paper. "Check it out, Mal," he said. Then he sat and stared back at Tony Swires, soaking up the man's bitterness and aggression, neither of them speaking.

Within a few minutes, Brady returned. "Checks out," he said grudgingly.

Neal thanked him with a nod. "Thanks for your co-operation, Mr Swires," he said. "You can go now. But I must ask you not to leave the building for the time being."

His features twisting in an ugly sneer of triumph, Swires noisily shoved back his chair and rose to his feet. "Try barking up the right tree next time, Sergeant," he snarled, as he turned on his heel and stalked out.

Neal sighed as the door slammed shut. He glanced up at Brady, who hadn't returned to his seat. "Pity," he said.

"We were both liking him for it, Gally. He seemed the type. And he certainly had it in for Sanderson."

"Yes. Unfortunately for us, though, I don't think he was lying when he said he didn't know Jerry Rudd."

"Should we double check with his mother?" Mal wondered. "Just in case she was covering up for him?"

Neal grinned mirthlessly. "And have a day out in Weston-Super-Mare," he said. "What, in late November? No, Mal, I think we've got to take this on the chin and move on. Better fetch in the next one."

He pushed back his chair, got up and walked to the window, looked down on the busy road beyond the warehouse, wondering where they might have gone wrong.

Brady's footsteps sounded behind him. "This is Mr Childers," he announced. "He's just this minute arrived."

Neal turned to greet the newcomer, arranging his glum features into a smile of welcome. Their gazes met simultaneously.

Gordon Childers seemed to freeze in the doorway, while Neal stared at him fixedly, for how long he had no idea, recognizing him immediately despite the beard and vaguely aware of Brady switching puzzled glances between them. It seemed as if time stood still.

He was in another warehouse now, catapulted back down the months and years, back there as he'd been so often, peering at that pale, terrified face seconds before the gun had boomed, before he'd had the wit to fling himself at Clyde and knock him out of the path of the bullet which had killed him. Before he could evade the second shot, which tore into his shoulder, blasting him off his feet into the pile of cardboard boxes which flew up into the air to rain down on top of him, endorsing his darkness, condemning him to the deep purgatory of the months which followed.

The Face: a face he'd never been able to forget.

Childers was first to react. His gaunt features contorted with shock, he shoved the bewildered Brady out of his way, turned and dashed across the adjacent room, past the startled faces of Braddon, Swires, Bob Sanderson and others. It might have been Bob's anxious voice which called after him, but by then Neal had returned to his senses, back in the here and now, following in hot pursuit after the fleeing Childers.

Someone was entering through the outer door, but Childers, with surprising strength, wrestled him out of the way. The man tumbled to the floor in a flurry of arms and legs, and Neal hurdled over him, determined that the killer he'd sought despairingly and for so long, the author of his personal nightmare, shouldn't escape his clutches for a third time.

Cars were parked at the front of the building, the reps' cars in which they'd arrived that morning. Childers was making for his, a mad hand snatching the keys from his pocket. But as he reached the car and looked back, he saw that Neal was a matter of a few yards away, bearing down on him.

With a desperate lunge, he was upon him, as Childers tried to pull open the car door. The keys spattered on the gravel, and the fugitive turned and swung a fist at his assailant. It was a wild, arcing punch, and Neal ducked it, retaining his hold on the man's other arm. Childers looked feral, eyes starting from his head, his thin face convulsed with fear. A second punch caught Neal on the side of the head, stunning him momentarily, forcing him to loosen his grip. He snatched at the man with his free arm, but Childers was almost away, and Neal's flailing hand fastened on to the sleeve of his jacket. The material ripped, but Childers had slithered away, stumbled, turned and headed for the nearby road.

Neal followed. A strong runner, he quickly narrowed the distance between them to a few feet. Childers sensed him bearing down, tried to run faster in his growing desperation. The road was busy with traffic, but he had no option other than to take his chance, his only opportunity for escape…

Neal pulled up on hearing the eldritch shriek of brakes, watched in horror as he saw his quarry bounce off the front of an oncoming van and collapse on to the road.

As he rushed forward to where the man lay, he heard a stampede of footsteps behind him, glimpsed a sea of bewildered faces: Mal, Mike Braddon, Swires, Sanderson and several others. The distraught driver tumbled out of his cab. "Honest, he just ran out in front of me. There was no way I could pull up in time…"

"Mal!" Neal yelled above the din. "Call an ambulance! Call Maddox and get some back-up!"

Dimly aware of Brady scuttling back towards the warehouse, Neal bent over the crumpled form of Gordon Childers. He felt for a pulse, found one. But it was very weak.

As the small crowd gathered round him, speechless, staring in disbelief at the body of their colleague, as the driver stood shocked and helplessly protesting, he found himself mumbling over and over, "Hurry, for God's sake, hurry. He can't die – he mustn't, mustn't die…"

The words kept tumbling out, a mantra of despair over which he had no control. Until the sound of sirens drew closer, and he realized Mal was at his shoulder, helping him to his feet and urging him to come away.

26

The ambulance and a squad car arrived within seconds of one another. Neal, returning to his senses, explained what had happened, going through it all again once DS Maddox showed up.

Mal Brady went with Childers to the hospital, while Neal and Maddox ushered the van driver into the building, followed by Mike Braddon and his staff. Braddon's secretary, an unflappable, middle-aged lady, made everyone tea, while Neal reassured the anxious van driver that someone would shortly arrive to take a statement, and that Neal would testify on his behalf that he wasn't to blame.

He could hear Braddon and the reps discussing the incident, voices shrill with incredulity, playing the same questions back and forth between them. *"Why did he run? How could it have been **Gordon** they were looking for? Whatever could he have done to make him bolt like that?"*

Bob Sanderson was unashamedly in tears, one of the other reps sitting with a comforting arm around him. Neal took Mike Braddon aside, fended off his questions and explained that Gordon Childers had been wanted for questioning with an incident in Oxford dating back almost three years. He'd recognized Neal from that time, had panicked and fled. Neal could give no more details, as he first needed to liaise with Cheltenham police.

Once everything was more or less under control, Maddox drove Neal back to Cheltenham police headquarters, where Neal explained everything once again for the benefit of Maddox's boss and then telephoned Don Pilling to put him in the picture, repeating the same story, his words droning, his brain scrambled.

Pilling, concerned for Neal, advised him to return to Oxford and let Maddox and his DCI, two very competent officers, take it from there.

"I'd like to stay for a while longer, Guv," Neal replied reasonably. "Brady's with him at the hospital. I'll send him back to Oxford and wait up there myself. I'd like to see this through."

He fully expected his Guv'nor to turn down his request, but Pilling, satisfied that Neal had got himself under control, gave his permission, requesting full verbal and written reports the next day.

Neal thanked him, then phoned Jill to say he'd be late back but couldn't offer any further details. He informed Maddox that Brady would return to Oxford in the car in which they'd arrived, and his fellow DS offered to organize a lift back home for Neal when he was ready.

*

It was evening by the time the Cheltenham squad car dropped Neal off at his flat. Jill had been looking out for him and came down to meet him at the front door. Closing it behind him, he stood and held her tightly for a long while before they climbed the stairs to the flat. Jill had kept a meal heated up for him, and he ate it, realizing he'd had nothing since leaving the flat early that morning.

As they sat together over mugs of tea, he told her the full story, and she listened intently, understanding that, while a longstanding issue had finally been resolved and the case closed, the events of the day had affected him deeply.

"Did he say anything at the end?" she asked.

"He seemed to know who I was and turned towards me. It was hardly a turn of the head, given the bandages and the condition he was in. His eyes were misting over – they'd given him something to ease the pain. Speech was difficult for him, and I only just caught the words, but he said that he was sorry and asked if I would forgive him. I did. I heard myself speaking words I could never have said if I'd caught up with him in the normal run of things. But of course, I couldn't answer for the others: Clyde, Terry Arden, Jerry Rudd. He seemed satisfied with that, and I sat and held his hand as he slipped away."

"Did you have any idea before today that he was almost within reach?" Jill wondered.

"He wasn't on my radar at all. He was just the Face, as distant as he'd ever been. I was fully focused on this case, sure that Tony Swires was our man. It's so easy with hindsight, but I've been over it time and again. Gordon Childers killed Terry Arden because of the gun Arden had passed on to him. Arden had used it to carry out those corner shop hold-ups before selling it on to Childers. We'll never know why Childers used it to hold up Mr Hobbs, nor why he was so desperate for money at that time. Arden had been into gambling, or so we learned after his death. Had he got Childers into it and then into debt?"

"But where did Jerry Rudd come in?"

"Colin Trevis sold Arden the gun one night in the Blue Dahlia. We had a witness who confirmed Childers was with Arden, and Rudd must have been there and recognized him the next time he ran into him. Jerry had a memory for faces, and he'd have stored up that knowledge in case it proved useful. When we were trying to track down that gun, Rudd must have somehow traced or run into Childers and asked him to inform Arden that we were on his trail regarding those hold-ups.

"I'd guess Rudd was looking for a pay-day from Arden, because he'd been so helpful in tipping him off about our interest. But then he must have realized he'd somehow spooked Childers, and that *he* had something to hide. Terry Arden, once we caught up with him, would have been able to identify Childers as the man to whom he'd passed the gun which was later used on Clyde and me. So, Childers had to remove Arden before we got to him, which he did.

"He was in Jerry's clutches then. Rudd blackmailed him, knowing he had something to hide, but probably not what. In any case, he wasn't going to let him forget, and in his desperation, Childers offered up to Rudd's tender mercies his one, true friend – Bob Sanderson, who was carrying on with a married woman.

"Rudd blackmailed the woman, Avril Walden, and when she couldn't keep up the payments, turned his sights back on Gordon Childers. Childers stole Sanderson's car, arranged to meet Rudd and killed him, throwing suspicion on to Sanderson. He'd probably have been happier to have implicated Tony Swires, a fellow rep and difficult character with a permanent chip on his shoulder, but Swires was miles away and in any case had an alibi for the night of Rudd's murder."

*

Towards the end of the following week, Jill accompanied Neal to Gloucester, where they attended Gordon Childers' cremation. It was a brief, impersonal service, with only a handful of his colleagues present. Childers' parents didn't attend, and it had taken Neal some time to trace them. They belonged to a strict religious sect and had disowned their only son many years previously. Neal had a very basic understanding of the Christian faith, but the way he understood it, it was about forgiveness and compassion, not hard-heartedness and judgement.

Bob Sanderson was present, with Avril Walden beside him. He looked pale and devastated, stunned at the way the man who'd been his friend had betrayed him.

Neal was glad of Jill's support, as must Bob have been of Avril's. Without her, he'd have felt drained, floundering around in a void.

"It's over," she said, as they walked back arm in arm to the car. "We can draw a line under it now."

With her beside him, he knew he could move on. The memories lingered, not so much of Clyde, because justice had been served, but more of Childers, 'the Face', and all the hatred Neal had felt over the last three years. He wondered about the point of it, or the point of hating someone at all, as he'd capitulated to hold the hand of his enemy as he'd slipped away.

He believed Childers had regretted all he'd done. He hadn't been able to summon up the courage to confess, as he'd stumbled through two more killings into a trap of his own making, baited with his fear, which had been forever lying in wait to confound and overwhelm him.

Neal found sleep difficult that night. He left Jill sleeping peacefully and went through to the adjoining room. As he sat there in the silence, he wondered if he should feel a sense of triumph with three murders solved and the case finally closed. He felt none and was glad he'd be returning to work the next day to tackle something new.

He recalled Jill's words, when she'd spoken to him about Anne Barcham. *"Everyone has their story."* What had been Gordon Childers' story? What were the circumstances which had led him to do what he'd done? And how had he let his fear consume him to the point where he'd thrown away the precious gift of the friendship of the one man who'd looked up to him?

As the bleak November day stirred into life, Neal sat deep in thought, feeling a sadness he'd not long ago have reckoned impossible, as he bowed his head and prayed for him.

*

The Baited Trap, copyright Michael Limmer 2025.

If you've enjoyed reading this book…

why not try one of Michael Limmer's other titles, listed at the front of this book? Several are available through Amazon as paperback and Kindle e-book. Otherwise, contact mike_limmer@yahoo.com for a full list of titles.

MARLA

"Warn Marla."

A dying man's last words…

But is she still alive?

And if so, where is she?

Someone knows more than they're prepared to tell and, as Glen Preston searches for clues in Marla's distant past, that someone is determined at all costs to prevent him from finding out…